PRAISE FOR DAN

Carter and Sophie's story kept me burning through the pages.

Wow! Danielle Norman certainly knows how to make you feel all the feels when she writes a book. I could not put Almost, her second book in her Iron Orchids series, down. I love how she is able to write a complete stand alone, while creating a world you never want to leave.

— ✩✩✩✩✩ AMAZON REVIEWER

5 Sexy, Fun and Fabulous Debut Stars!!!

One of the biggest joys I have as a reader is finding a new author, whether to me or a brand new author with their debut novel. My friends, I'm here to tell you that Danielle Norman is an author you NEED in your life.

— ✩✩✩✩✩ AMAZON REVIEWER

SOPHIE, ALMOST MINE

Iron Orchids

DANIELLE NORMAN

Reviews are Important

HEY, don't forget to leave a review when you're done reading. Here are perks exclusive to Danielle fans only, bwahaha

AT 250 REVIEWS- you get a lifetime subscription of the sugar free, knock-off version of Oreos called Whoreos. Did you read that wrong? It is Who reos, get your mind out of the gutter.

AT 500 REVIEWS- Tiny leprechauns dressed up as Thunder Down Under give live performances FREE for all of my fans.

AT 1000 REVIEWS- A UNICORN jumps out of every book and lulls you to sleep with a lullaby before shanking anyone that karma forgot with its horn.

When writing a story about a seventeen-year-old girl getting pulled over by a sheriff, I figured that I better dedicate this to the actual deputy that pulled me over when I was seventeen. Play theme song to Silence of the Lambs and Hand That Rocks the Cradle. Anyway, you weren't really creepy, you were just in your mid-twenties, and I was SEVENTEEN! Of course, when you told me to get out of my car on the night of my eighteenth birthday we only kissed. So I'd like to thank you for the memories. Here's to my ability to exaggerate and exploit my fucked-up childhood adventure and to you for being a pervy stalker dude in a uniform. Cheers motherfucker.

And to my Mana, I miss you every day. But with the above dedication (confession) and the fact that I'm now writing books that go well with vodka and vibrators, I tell my heart that this is the world's way of righting itself.

"It's amazing how fast someone can become a stranger."

— ANONYMOUS

PROLOGUE

Carter

*S*ix years ago . . .

THE SOUND of chatter pulled me from my drunken sun-filled haze, and I looked over to see a group of women in bikinis gathered at the other end of the bar.

Lowering my aviator glasses, I evaluated the group. Two ladies wore solitaire diamonds, which probably meant that they were engaged. One wore a wedding band, and one had no ring at all. Some things you couldn't take out of the guy, even on vacation and one of those was my natural sheriff instincts to notice the little things like ringless fingers.

Picking up my bottle, I took another swig before motioning to my server. I'd been in Vegas for just over twenty-four hours, and I hadn't been without a beer since. I wasn't going to start now. As long as I didn't switch to hard liquor, I would be fine. Liquor made me stupid, and I intended to spend my vacation shitfaced not smashed in the face by an angry husband for making some dumbass move on his wife. That didn't mean I wasn't going to spend a good bit of my time finding a few one-night stands. Provided they didn't expect anything. And they had no problem keeping their last name to themselves. I didn't do last names. Last names were for girls you planned to keep around. I had a motto: girls were like dessert. You savored dessert, you made room for dessert, but you did not eat the same dessert every night for the rest of your fucking life.

A shadow fell over me, and I looked up to see a server had finally made her way over.

"It's almost lunch, can I get you something?" She looked like she had been at this job for way too many years and probably had the stories to go with it.

"Sure, yeah. I'll take a burger."

"You got it, love. I'll be right back."

She had just left when another shadow fell over me, but this one was accompanied by the smell of coconut. I turned to see the woman that I spied earlier, the one without a ring, spreading out her towel on the chaise lounge next to mine. As she bent over, her artfully sculpted ass wiggled in my face. I mentally counted the seconds, any moment it would happen, it was a guaranteed pick-up line . . .

"Would you rub some lotion on my back? I can't reach."

BAM there it was.

Did women realize the thoughts that went through a man's mind when they asked that question? Sure, we didn't have a problem putting lotion on a woman's back, but it wasn't suntan lotion that we were thinking of. No, we were thinking that we'd like to put a white, man-made kind all over her instead.

Shrugging, I grabbed the bottle of Banana Boat and squirted some in my hands as she scooched closer, settling between my legs. My cock, which was always up for a good time, made sure his presence was noted.

"I think you were on my flight yesterday. Are you from Orlando?" Her smooth voice held no hint of an accent.

"Yep." I rubbed the lotion down her arms.

"I'm here for a bachelorette party, but after tonight, I'm free. I'm staying here for another two weeks. Need to use up my vacation time. How about you?"

"Something like that. I'll be here for a while as well, just hanging out by the pool."

"If you're not meeting anyone here, maybe we can get together. Two Floridians living it up in Vegas."

"You know where to find me," I said, giving her no promises as I finished her back.

The waitress interrupted us with my order and cleared away my empty bottle. I wiped my hands off on my towel before reaching up and signing the slip to charge the food order to my room. When I turned to offer the woman sitting next to me a French fry, she was gone. I couldn't help but smile, her game of seduction was nicely executed.

It didn't take long for the effects of jet lag, sunshine, and alcohol to wear on me, and in no time, I was practically comatose. Around four o'clock, like the party animal I was, I decided it was time for a nap, so I headed up to my room.

I didn't wake up until the next morning.

Prior to this trip, I hadn't been to Vegas, and since the Orange County Sheriff's Department was forcing me to take two weeks of vacation before I transitioned into my new position on motors, I figured this was the best place for a single guy to find women, alcohol, women, gambling, women, so on and so forth.

So, since I at least had a clear mission, I took a quick shower, got dressed, and headed downstairs. Exiting the elevator, I turned to the left and then headed through the casino to the other side for the restaurants. The pyramid shape of the Luxor was intriguing but much larger than it appeared from the outside. The place was a fucking maze to top all mazes, and I was damn tempted to leave breadcrumbs so I could find my way back. Maybe they should consider putting colored lines on the floor, blue takes you to the pool, green to the casino where you will lose all of your green, and red for food . . .

Finally finding a small bistro, I ordered steak and eggs and sat in silence and ate. I was just finishing when the sound of moans pulled me from my sleepy state.

"Hey. . ." The girl from yesterday groaned as she lowered her sunglasses and tried to take me in. She looked like the rest of her friends—well, to be honest, she looked like several women I'd already seen on this bright Sunday morning. Her hair was messy and piled atop her head, black makeup smudged under her eyes, and she was trying to shake off the effects of last night's alcohol.

"Shhh," her friend chided her for groaning too loud.

"Last night was the bachelorette party?"

"Yeah."

"Looks like you all had fun."

"I think so, can't remember." She held her head as if trying to balance herself.

"Well, I'm headed out to the pool, and hopefully, I will be in a can't-remember-shit state of mind very soon as well. Have fun." I stood and waved goodbye but before I was through the doorway leading back toward the slot machines, I turned back. Yup, she and her friends were watching me. I smiled and gave them a slight salute before continuing on my way, snagging a towel from the cabana, and grabbing the same seat as yesterday.

Just after lunch, the ringless woman joined me, and that night, I didn't sleep alone.

For the next ten days, we drank, caught a few shows, drank, gambled, drank some more, and fucked like rabbits.

I was leaving in the morning, and she still had two more days there, but honestly, I didn't care if she stayed in this city forever. We had kept it casual as promised, and I wouldn't see her again. That night we headed out with a Club Crawl map and cash in our pockets. We started at the Light Bar and then hit the Foundation Room before spending some time at Coyote Ugly. The louder the music, the busier the crowds, the more we drank. Laughing, we recounted all of the crazy things we had done in Vegas, thank God that what happened there stayed there. Trying to get in any last-minute things that we could think of, we ran up to the registration desk at Caesars Palace and asked if Caesar had actually stayed there in an imitation of Zach Galifianakis from the Hangover.

"Is this hotel pager friendly?" she asked, and I cracked up laughing for some stupid reason. Knowing that we weren't going to get "roofied" or "flooried" as they referred to them in the movie since we were more likely to end up on the floor rather than the roof. We set out to relive the movie.

In the city that never shuts down, we drank our way up and down the strip. With the exception of the tiger we couldn't think of anything else to do from the movie, so we finally called it a night, well morning since the sun was breaking the horizon.

We found our way back to the Luxor—how I had no fucking clue. Once inside the elevator, I tried to press the button while trying to hold myself up. I fucking couldn't find the button to my hotel floor. Fuck. Where was it? I leaned down to look at the teeny tiny illuminated circles.

One of those bastards had to have had a fourteen on it.

Eventually, all the lights were fucking lit up, so it didn't matter. It wasn't my fault they made the damn things too small for anyone to read.

Finally making my way to the hallway and eventually my room, I pulled out my key card, sliding the damn thing in and out of the lock until the green light finally came on. I let go of Ivey's hand for just a second to help her inside before the door clicked behind us.

Chapter One

SOPHIE

The siren wailed, I looked into my rearview mirror just as the sheriff's car closed in behind me and flipped on its lights. Shit. I slowed and drove just past the turnoff to my subdivision, the last thing I needed was someone seeing me get pulled over. Glancing at the clock on the giant center gauge in my MINI Cooper, it was barely past midnight, but it was officially my birthday. I put my car in park and waited for his approach. Looking around I had this sinking feeling in my stomach, that sense of apprehension that something was about to happen. This part of the road was deserted with no streetlights. For a second, I seriously considered calling Carter; he was a deputy, after all. Then I remembered that he wasn't working this area tonight, so he wouldn't be much help.

Damn it, Sophie, you should've stayed in a well-lit area. I was bitching myself out about my bad decision, knowing full well that it was too little too late. My mental lecture was interrupted by the man's voice that came across a PA system. "Turn off the engine and step out of your car."

My legs went numb, I threw my head back against the

headrest and tried to take this all in as I fumbled to unbuckle my seatbelt. Oh, my God. This wasn't right. It couldn't be. Something was wrong. This wasn't normal protocol. Unclasping my seatbelt was one of those things I did without thinking, but tonight it took every bit of brainpower just to find the damn button. Free from the restraint, I slid out from my vehicle.

"Close the door. Place your hands on your head and face away from me," the steely voice ordered across the PA.

The beat of my heart increased, and I was positive that at any moment it was going to explode. I'd seen cops do things like that in movies just before they hauled the person off to jail. Only, I hadn't done anything. There had to be some mistake. As I stood waiting in the dark with only the flickering lights behind me, eeriness seemed to surround me, and I started to panic at the thought that the man who just ordered me out of my car might not be an actual cop. Maybe he was a serial killer. I'd read about stuff like that happening, where some guy stole a car and then pulled over innocent people just to rape them or chop them up. I silently pleaded for God to please not let anything happen to me. I'd do anything—I'd be a better person, I'd start volunteering more, I'd go to church every week—if only I didn't end up in jail or dead.

Feet crunched on the gravel shoulder of the road as the officer got closer. My body was electrified with the combination of fear and anticipation. Would he handcuff me? Taser me?

In an instant, his hands were on me, spinning me around until I was face to face with Officer Carter Lang. "Happy eighteenth birthday, Sophie," he whispered as he pulled a small wrapped box from his pocket . . .

Another voice came across a PA system, this one waking me up. "Ladies and gentleman, please return your seats and tray tables to their upright position as we prepare for our descent into the Orlando International Airport."

Apparently, I'd slept the entire flight from California. Pressing my hands against the armrests, I took several rapid breaths. That damn flight attendant. That motherfucking flight attendant. My dream was just getting to the good part. I rocked in my seat, remembering Carter's smooth hand as he slid it into my—

The plane jerked as it touched down, braking to a speed slow enough to roll to the gate. I waited for the chime that signaled it was safe to remove my seatbelt before standing and grabbing my overhead bag. I stood in the aisle fidgeting, shifting my weight from leg to leg waiting for the slow-as-fuck attendants to open the damn plane door.

I couldn't believe myself, that dream, even after ten years, he still filled my every fucking fantasy.

Maneuvering my way off the plane, I headed for the tram that would take me to the main concourse. People raced by me, I never understood why people ran, and scrunched in, climbing over each other as if this were the very last tram of the fucking day. Trying to keep my carry-on close against me, some asshat jumped in just as the doors were closing, causing the surrounding people to stumble. As everyone righted themselves and held on, the doors closed and we moved. A buzzing sound echoed around us filling the small acoustic car.

Buzzzzzzzz.

Heads turned as we all tried to find the culprit. A slow burn crept up my cheeks for whoever's bag was going off, I could only imagine the humiliation boiling inside of them at this very moment. I mean, come on, it was obviously a vibrator. A quick glance around lets me know that clearly, I wasn't the only one who thought so by the number of people grinning. Men in business suits were smirking and women were snickering.

A little boy near me knelt down to the front of my suitcase before looking up at me. And in his little boy voice that was too loud for such a small space said, "Lady, your bag is humming." I froze as all heads turned to stare at me. What? There was no way. I didn't travel with a vibrator, there was no way in hell I was having a TSA agent find something like that in my bag.

"Can't be mine." I dismissed the kid hoping that he'd go away.

"It's your bag." He placed his hand on my suitcase. "Mommy come feel, it's her bag."

Everyone watched me as I wracked my brain for what in the fuck could be vibrating, and the realization hit, my toothbrush. My motherfucking Crest Spinbrush toothbrush.

"Oh shit, it's my toothbrush."

"Surrre." I heard one man say as others laughed at his comment.

I shot daggers at him. "No, I'm serious. It really is, it has to be." Just as I was bending to unzip my bag and pull it out, the monorail came to a stop and people started to file off. In a last-ditch effort, I finally got my hand on the vibrating culprit and pulled it out, waving it in the air as if it were the baton for the relay at the motherfucking Olympics. But unfortunately, most people had moved on, leaving me as the lone survivor in the security area. I was sure there was some agent watching me on camera waving my toothbrush and wondering what the hell I was doing. Turning it off and then shoving it back in my bag, I swore to never travel with a vibrating toothbrush again.

I walked out of the secure area and headed toward ground transportation. Opening my phone, I sent a text to my cousin Ian to let him know that I was there. When I headed through the sliding doors, the squawking honk of a horn had me smiling at the silver sports car pulling up to the curb.

"Look at you, all grown up," Ian said as he got out of his car and walked around to give me a hug before grabbing my bag and putting it in his trunk.

"You look sharp. It's amazing how much we change in ten years, isn't it?" I replied.

As Ian drove, I stared out the window, trying to see if Orlando felt different. Would I recognize everything or would the place be a circus?

"What's that big Ferris Wheel?"

"The Orlando Eye, kind of like the London Eye. See where it is?"

I nodded. "Yeah, is that International Drive?"

"Yup. What's someone going to see over there anyway, air conditioner units on the top of buildings? I can't understand why they built that wheel there. Why not closer to Kennedy Space Center so people can see the ocean, the Space Shuttle, and actual pieces of American history?"

"You wouldn't happen to be biased because you are a rocket scientist, would you?"

"Be quiet."

Smiling, I turned back to the window and peered out at the passing landscape. This place, this town that I had always considered home, wasn't any longer. I was the outsider. Twisting my head back and forth as I tried to take in all of the changes that surrounded me. The construction along Interstate 4 seemed to go on for miles. I wanted to get in my car and drive just to explore the town that at one time was my comfort place.

Ian turned onto Pente Loop. The last time I was here Ian's dad, George, had just finished building my cousin Damon's house, and now my other three cousins had homes along this same street as well. About midway down was a new street. I smiled when Ian turned into a driveway. My Uncle owned a construction company and had built my mom a pretty white stone house with pillars and a gray slate roof.

"Your mom has been dying to see you, she's really missed you." He put his car in park and opened his door. "Go on in, I'll bring your bag."

I looked at my mom's house, which was where I would be staying until I found a place of my own. She'd always wanted me to live with her until I got married. At one time her dream was for me to stay close and have a house full of children. But it was time for me to grow up and be on my own. I loved her and wanted to live close by so wherever I moved it wouldn't be far.

I'd stayed with her in California since she bought a large house when I was going through a bad time in my life and wanted to take care of me. But, moving back to Orlando was the perfect time for me to step out on my own.

Twisting the knob on the front door, I walked in and was greeted to the smell of honey, lemon, and Mediterranean spices, which made my stomach grumble even though I wasn't hungry. It was the fragrance of home. Feeling Ian's hand on my shoulder he escorted me out of the doorway and toward the back of the house to the kitchen.

"Aunt Dion, we're here!" he yelled.

"You're here. How was your flight?"

"Long. Taking the red eye sucks plus losing three hours, ugh."

"I'll leave and let you two catch up," Ian said. "I've got to head into the office." He leaned down and gave my mom a kiss on her cheek and then gave me a hug. "Glad to have you home, Soph."

"Thanks, it's good to be home. Thank you for the ride."

I smiled up at him and it was like looking in a mirror, our eyes were the same shade of brown, our skin the same olive tone. Most of my life people assumed that I was the baby sister of the Christakos family instead of the cousin. But, since I was the only female cousin, I couldn't imagine being the sister would be much different, the guys were protective and overbearing.

My mom reached for my hand and pulled me to her table. "I took the day off. Are you hungry, I can fix you something."

"No, I'm fine. How do you like being back in the Orlando office?" I asked. My mom worked for Disney, and ten years ago when she transferred out to Anaheim, it was only supposed to be for a year. I was going to stay in Orlando and start college at UCF until she came back. But life never seemed to work out the way we intended. She ended up staying out there to take care of me. So, when the opportunity for her to move back was offered, I agreed to move with her. If I hadn't she would had stayed in California and been torn. I couldn't do that to her, she'd already given up so much for me.

"I love being back. Totally new buildings but so many of the same people. It's nice being here, it's home. Plus, I love having our family this close. Your Uncle George and Aunt Christine constantly come by, and I haven't had to hire anyone to mow the yard since one of the boys always comes by and does it. It's amazing having guy help and not having to hire it." She laughed. "And wait until you see your house."

"My house? I haven't started looking yet."

A wide smile spread across my mother's cheeks from holding back her laughter. "George is an idiot," Mom said. "But I love him dearly. It seems he took it upon himself to help you with that."

I followed my mom out her front door and toward her neighbor's house. It was a two-story yellow Victorian home, a life-size Barbie house with blue shingles that looked like fish scales. There was a giant wrap-around porch complete with a swing and rocking chairs. Peaked turrets were balanced on either side and a balcony in the middle.

"Obviously some full-time princess lives here," I said, gesturing to the gorgeous monstrosity.

"According to your Uncle, the princess of the family will live here. You. That's your house."

"Seriously?" I knew my jaw was hanging open a bit, but I couldn't help it.

Walking up to the front door, a small pang of loneliness squeezed my heart. This house was so large and it was just me, only me, all by myself, would only ever be me. But at the same time my insides were stirring because this house—oh my God, I had my own house— it was so large. There was no way that I'd ever fill it.

Pushing open the ornate wooden door, the scent of cinnamon and oranges wafted through the air and a pair of familiar green eyes met mine. Frozen at the threshold while I tried to take in the brunette with a pixie cut who was wearing biker boots and a Harley Davidson T-shirt. Although we hadn't spoken since we graduated from high school, I'd recognize her anywhere. As if no time had passed, I threw my arms around her and basked in the realization that I was home.

My mom scooted around us and headed deeper into the house.

"Before you say anything," my best friend since kindergarten said, "I had my name legally changed to Leo."

I took a step back and checked her out from head to toe. "No more hideous skirts?" I asked.

Leo shook her head.

"No more weird religious shit that your mom shoves down our throats?"

Leo shook her head.

"And I can't call you Leono—" My words were cut off by her hand covering my mouth.

"No. Absolutely not. I am just Leo."

"I don't care what you call yourself, I am just happy to see you. I have missed you so much."

"Come on, let me introduce you to the others." Leo led me into my house and right past my suitcase, which hadn't even occurred to me that Ian hadn't brought it into my mom's house when he dropped me off.

In a rush of movement, two hands cupped my face and my head was forcibly tilted to the left, right, and back as Aunt Christine examined me close up. "It's so good to see you! You are too thin." She kissed my cheeks and walked back to wherever she came from.

Ahh, it was good to be home.

"We've been unpacking all of the boxes that your mom said were yours plus all the shit she and your Aunt Christine have bought you. The place is pretty well equipped."

"Who's 'we'?"

A loud cough came from a woman stacking dishes on a shelf. "Sophie, this is Stella."

"The one and only. I've heard a lot about you." Stella stopped putting stuff away to meet me.

A redhead stood next to her, smile beaming, and I knew exactly who she was. "And you must be Ariel," I said. "I am so glad to finally meet you. We've talked so much on the phone that I feel as if we know each other." I wrapped her in a tight hug as if we'd been friends forever. She was engaged to my cousin Kayson, to Greeks that made her family.

"Let's take a break." Ariel's Southern drawl was heavy and endearing. It didn't take much for everyone to abandon their tasks.

I followed Leo and Stella over to a table where boxes of donuts were set out next to a carafe of coffee.

"Leo, you're here, in my house, with my family and soon

to be family, how?" I asked, shocked, never expecting to see my childhood best friend still involved with my family.

"I'm a mechanic. Well, actually a Harley Davidson mechanic. Kayson brought his bike in one day, and we recognized each other from all the times you and I were together." Leo grabbed a donut and took a bite. "I met Ariel at a Harley event when she and Kayson reconnected and Stella's brother is a motorcycle deputy with Kayson which is how I met Stella."

I poured a cup of coffee, I was operating on very little quality sleep, and I didn't want to be rude and yawn while Leo was explaining how they had all connected so I loaded up on caffeine.

"In fact, it was at that event we decided to form an all-girls motorcycle club." The three of them laughed at some inside joke that I was obviously missing. "You know had we not met that night and formed our club, I wouldn't be roped into helping you with your damn ball," Leo said with a groan to Ariel but I could tell that she was teasing.

"Oh, you love me, admit it." Ariel puckered up and pretended that she was going to give Leo a giant kiss. "Well, I'm so happy that Sophie agreed to be a participant for the fundraiser at the ball. It is going to be amazing." Ariel gave Stella a weird look, her excitement over having my help with the ball seemed a little over the top. She reminded me of a spastic Pomeranian at that moment. Maybe it was just me because I was tired but I had this strange feeling that she and Stella were exchanging a silent conversation that I wasn't privy to.

"I'm honored that you asked," I replied a little skeptically as I watched her and Stella. "I love doing events, but most of the time, the events are full of kids. It will be a nice change of pace to get to talk to adults." I'd been rehearsing that line, confident it was how I'd feel under normal circumstances.

But not for this ball where Ariel decided it would be fun to hold an auction and the prize was me. I'd already committed to her event and my cousin was so appreciative of me helping her that I didn't dare back out or I would have found a million and one ways to still be in California until after her ball.

"Not just adults. Adult cops. Let me tell you how hot some of the officers—" Stella was cut off by a sharp elbow to the ribs.

"Cool it, Stella." Leo smiled and nodded to my mom, who was eyeing us as if she knew exactly what Stella just said.

Ariel just laughed. "Well, they are all excited to meet Kayson's cousin. You're apparently the talk of the station."

"Yeah?"

"Yeah. Stella's brother said that the guys have been relentless. They all want to know where he's been hiding you."

I fell silent, knowing that I hadn't really been hiding but that my disappearing without a word was still hard on my whole family.

I managed a smile. "Well, I'm back. So, no more mystery, right?"

"Right," Leo said. "And you can prove that by coming to Sixes with us tonight."

"Sounds like a plan." I had no idea what or where that was, but if my alternative was to hang out at this house alone, then I'd take them up on the invitation.

"Sophie, are you listening?" Ariel waved her hand in front of my face, pulling me from my thoughts.

"I'm sorry, what?"

"I said that you are going to love your office, wait until you see it." She stood. "Come on, let me show you." The four of us walked out of the kitchen and down a hall to a room that was clearly part of the turret. Though, from inside it was more of a hexagon shape with windows on every wall except one, that wall held French doors that opened up to the porch with a swing. "I can see you writing your opus there." Ariel pointed to the desk that overlooked the backyard.

"You do understand that I write children's books, for little children, right? My books aren't exactly the great American novels. Little kids don't have that kind of attention span."

"I don't care. It is still an inspiring room. I picked out the furniture," Ariel defended with a smile, confident that I was going to be inspired here.

"It is gorgeous, thank you. You have excellent taste."

"Well, I don't give a rat's ass about the office." Stella flicked her wrist dismissing Ariel's airy thought of writing grandeur. "I want to talk about Sophie officially becoming part of our gang."

"We're not a gang," Ariel and Leo corrected Stella.

"Oh, whatever." Stella ignored them.

"What is she talking about?" I gave Ariel and Leo a what-the-fuck look because I was totally lost.

"We"—Ariel pointed to herself then to Leo and Stella —"are part of an all ladies motorcycle club called the Iron Orchids. There are six of us right now. But we're hosting a ladies only class in just over a week. And we'd love for you to come."

"Yes. Yes. Yes," Leo pleaded, now she was resembling the spastic Pomeranian.

"It'll be fun. And since you and Ariel are practically family and you and Leo were obviously super close, that means we will be hanging out together a lot anyway," Stella explained as if that was reason alone for me to join a gang.

I couldn't get over the fact that these women rode motor-cycles, it seemed so gritty and manly. I was a sundress and three-hundred-dollar ballet flats kind of girl, not a Harley woman.

"Just think about it. Come to class, you never know." Ariel headed out of my office and back toward the kitchen.

I let out a yawn.

"You are coming with us tonight, right?" Leo questioned.

"Yeah, but I'd like to drive just in case I get exhausted and want to come home early."

"How about if I come by here and you can follow me?" Ariel asked, offering up the perfect solution since she lived with my cousin Kayson less than a block away.

"Sounds good," I replied between yawns.

"Let's get out of here and you can get some rest. I'll swing by just before seven."

Hugging the girls goodbye, I escorted them to my front door and waited for them to leave before making my way into the kitchen to where my mom and aunt were busily talking.

"I need to sleep." I bent and gave each one a kiss on their cheek before heading back out of the kitchen. I stopped in the doorway. "Umm, where's my bedroom?"

The soft chuckle came from my mom before she said, "Upstairs and to the left." My mom pointed using two fingers, her trained, Disney-style way of giving directions.

THE BEST WAY for me to describe Sixes was to call it a taverna, it was part tavern, part restaurant. It had that distinct smell of fried food, wooden tables, and beer. The sounds of Adele rolled through the air as a DJ stationed up front kept music going. There was a parquet dance floor in the center, and a few pool tables off to one side. Walls held T-shirts from local law enforcement officers and helmets from local fire stations.

Ariel headed for the table in the corner where Leo, Stella, and a few other ladies I hadn't met yet were already sitting.

"Everyone, this is Sophie; Sophie, this is everyone," Leo said as way of introduction.

"Hi, I'm Piper, I work with Kayson at the sheriff's office." A pretty woman with strawberry blonde hair held out her hand.

Just as I pulled out a chair, a waitress came by and set a tray of shot glasses filled with all kinds of liquid in the center of the table. She informed us that the food would be right out, and then strode away to fill another order.

"Here," Stella said, as she handed each of us a pink shot before I had a chance to meet the other ladies. "To Sophie coming home." Everyone clinked their glasses and slammed their drink back. As they say "When in Rome."

Hot wings and fries were delivered first, followed by cheese sticks and sliders a few minutes later.

"We all chip in at the end, so just grab what you want," Leo whispered in my ear, obviously reading my confusion of the groups dining etiquette. Thankful, I nodded and then slid an appetizer plate closer before reaching for a slider.

"Hey, I need all of you to give me your advice. There is this new dumbass doctor running the ICU, and he hates me. I think that I need to switch floors." Stella's demeanor changed; she looked serious for the first time since I had met her that morning.

"First, just tell me, what did you do now?" Leo asked.

"He told me that I'm intimidating. Me? What the fuck? Me intimidating?"

"What did you say when he told you that?" Ariel's smirk was enough to tell me that something was up, either Stella got into trouble a lot or there was a punchline coming.

"Nothing, I just stared at him until he apologized."

I looked around our table, was she serious? I couldn't contain it any longer, I burst out laughing. "You are whacked." I leaned across the table and squeezed Stella's hands.

"How long did it take you to come up with that joke? Girl you have more lines than AT&T," Ariel said between hoots of laughter.

Any moment I was going to need some Dramamine from the motion sickness of going back and forth. They were a tennis match volleying their quips, but I loved the bond that was clearly evident and was a bit jealous. Leo had always been my best friend but I'd abandoned her just like I had. . .

"Don't worry about it, Stella's an acquired taste," Leo said as she gave Stella a bright smile.

"You know what else is an acquired taste?" Stella replied drawing me back into their banter.

"Nooo." Leo threw her hands up over her ears. "We're eating and don't need to discuss your sexual escapades."

Stella let out an evil sounding cackle. "Just remember young Padawan, I always get the last word."

Except for my editor, who lived in New York, I pretty much didn't talk to anyone in my job, I was alone most of the time. Writing on the whole was a lonely career and it didn't leave a ton of opportunities to meet people outside of the business. And since my fans were kids, it cut my connections even smaller.

"Are you ready for Saturday night?" Ariel leaned over and bumped my shoulder.

"As ready as a lamb being led to slaughter." I mean, come on, what did she expect me to say? "Yay, I'm so excited that you are going to be auctioning me off for dinner and dancing to some sheriff's deputy. Oh, by the way, there is a high probability of one of those guys being Carter, a guy I haven't talked to in ten years but still dream about."

Yeah, no. That wasn't going to happen.

Chapter Two

CARTER

$\mathcal{I}$ headed out of the station and got on my bike to go home. I was officially on vacation, and I was going to do everything in my power to avoid the woman that I knew had arrived today. Making a mental list of all the ways to keep me from searching for her, I decided to head to the community center in the morning, that would take a lot of my time and keep me away from Sophie. Arriving home to my quiet two-bedroom first floor without a view condo, I quickly changed out of my uniform. Most people would complain about windows that overlooked the parking garage but not me, since I didn't have to pay condominium fees. Provided I was with the sheriff's department and agreed to park my marked unit in the front spot, which was reserved for me. The property management company thought that it deterred criminals. Most of my neighbors were elderly, and I tried to visit them when I could to fix anything they needed or just change out lightbulbs.

I walked a few doors down, to Mrs. Goodwin's condo. She was a neighbor that I checked in with even on days like today when I wasn't in the mood or didn't have time to make my rounds to everyone else. For her, I always found time to visit. She was my favorite. Hell, she even had a key to my place and frequently came over and cleaned. While she was there she would iron my uniforms and stock my fridge with home cooked meals. At first, I tried to object but realized that she needed it as much as I truly needed having someone do it. I gave my standard shave and haircut knock.

"Is that my Carter boy? Come in here. I haven't seen you in forever."

"It's only been a week."

"But to an old woman like me, that's forever. You never know how many days you have left."

I let out a laugh. Mrs. Goodwin was probably going to outlive everyone. "I just stopped by to see if you needed anything. I'm on vacation this week. Orange County is on spring break, so I'll be trying to put in some extra hours at the community center."

"Boy, you are too good. Why haven't you met a girl yet?" Her words struck me deep. I had met a girl, but then that girl up and disappeared. "What's that look on your face for? Did you meet someone? Come on in and tell me all about it. I just made some fresh oatmeal cookies, and I was packing some up for you. I know they're your favorite."

I walked into her kitchen, spotted a burned out light bulb, and grabbed a new one from the shelf above her washing machine so I could change it for her. All the while, I thought of what to say. Mrs. Goodwin wouldn't let me leave without something. "May I ask, how long were you married?"

"Sixty-one years. Alfred and I met our first year of college."

"How long did you wait before you got married?"

"Oh, have you fallen madly in love with someone?" I shook my head, letting her know that wasn't it. "He asked me out on a date, and we were married eight months later. I just knew that he was the one. We had our fights over the years, some doozies. But no one ever gave me butterflies in my stomach like he did. Do you have butterflies, Carter?"

"I did but she left, and the butterflies just seemed to die."

"Can whatever it was that separated the two of you be fixed?"

"I don't know. Maybe I'm wrong. Maybe I've built it up to more than it really was, sometimes our mind plays tricks on us and remembers things that didn't really happen. It was ten years ago. She was seventeen, and I was twenty when we first met. It sounds stupid, I know."

Mrs. Goodwin's wrinkled hands clasped mine. "Alfred and I were eighteen, and after our first date I went home and told my mother that I had just met the man I was going to marry. So, no, it isn't stupid. I didn't find out for quite a few years that Alfred had gone to the jewelry store and bought my ring"—she pointed to the diamond that she still wore even though she'd been a widow for more than ten years—"after our third date. Carter, you go find that girl and see if the spark is still there. Your heart will let you know. The heart never lies."

Leaning over, I gave Mrs. Goodwin a peck on her cheek before grabbing the plastic container of cookies. "I'll get your container back to you in a day or two. You know how much I love your cookies, I'll go through these pretty fast." I left her apartment and headed back to mine, dropping the container on the counter before grabbing my keys and deciding to head up to Sixes to grab some dinner.

I had taken Mrs. Goodwin's words to heart and knew that it was only a matter of time before Sophie and I ran into each other. I just wasn't expecting it to be tonight and here, in my go-to place to relax. I looked up at the sound of my sister's laughter coming from the dance floor, but I wasn't focused on her, I was focused on the gorgeous woman a few feet behind her who was swaying to the song. I couldn't take my eyes off her.

Steadying myself against a table, I fought the lure that had pulled me in ten years ago, and still called to me after all these years. I closed my eyes, and my heart ached over all the nights we talked for hours on the phone, over the times we sat in the car and talked about nothing and everything. All those times I told her that I loved her but I couldn't show her because she wasn't eighteen . . . yet.

I took several deep breaths as I tried to regain my balance, remembering the way her smile used to light her eyes, and now as I looked closer, it seemed that her light was gone. It was replaced with a hint of sadness edging her eyes. She danced with abandon, and the words to the song "She Used To Be Mine" hit home.

I didn't want to make a scene, not here. Sixes was the favorite hangout for local law enforcement and most of the fire departments. In other words, I knew just about everyone. I seriously considered turning and sneaking back out but, my sister's voice stopped me.

"Well hell's bells. Yo, bro." I steeled myself, knowing those words were always followed by a five-foot-nine blonde cata-pulting herself onto my back like a fucking chimpanzee. And not letting me down, Stella leaped onto my back.

I swore to God the girl was never going to grow up. Anyone who saw the two of us next to each other would have no doubts that we were related. We had the same blond hair, blue eyes, height, and well . . . we just looked alike. Even though my sister was trying to get my attention, my focus wasn't on her, it was still on Sophie, who was talking with Leo and Piper. I wiggled my shoulders to extricate myself from Stella's grasp. I could hear Stella laughing as she jumped down but I ignored her, I was transfixed on the way Sophie's dark hair bobbed back and forth. I imagined wrapping it around my hand as I . . . shit . . . fuck . . . don't go there, Carter. There are people around but damn it all to hell, no one told my dick that he needed to worry about attracting attention. Oh no, he was at full attention remembering the night I had pulled her over and propped her sweet body up on the hood of her car. God, I still remembered the way she tasted when I licked my fingers. And of course, it was at that moment that Sophie turned to me, our eyes locked, and it hit me—Sophia Kostas had crushed me. The sound of my sister's heels stomping on the ground as she ran back to her friends sounded more like shots yanking me from my memories and replacing them with hurt and fury.

"Come on, you need to meet Kayson's cousin." Stella waved me toward her table where Sophie stood, our eyes still locked. "Sophie, this is my brother Carter."

She stretched out her hand. "You might not remember me." Her hand was shaking, and when she spoke there was a light quiver in her voice, it shattered her false image of assurance. "I know that it's been ten years." Her voice was still so soft and alluring. "And you may only remember me as the girl you used to pull over for speeding, but I valued our friendship and . . . well . . ."

"Only remember you as the girl I pulled over for speeding? Did I hear you right?" I couldn't control the ire that was slowly bubbling up inside me.

"Yeah, well . . . um."

A searing pain shot up my jaw as I clenched my teeth tight. "Sophia Christine Kostas born July fourteenth, lived on Skyline Drive in Kissimmee. You really think that I only remember you as the girl. Who. I. Pulled. Over. For. Speeding?"

"Wow, you have a great memory." She was being flippant after I spent ten years wondering what happened to her.

"You two know each other?" Leo interrupted.

Sophie stared at me, her eyes pleading for me to answer.

"Yeah, we know each other. Ten years ago, I worked patrol where Sophie lived, and we got to know each other because she tended to have a lead foot."

There were a few moments of silence as everyone tried to evaluate the volatility of the situation.

Sophie slid to the side. "I'm not feeling well. I'm going to head home. Talk to all of you later." Sophie dropped her head and shielded her eyes as she passed me and headed out the door.

Without a word to the women all staring after Sophie, I turned and followed her to the parking lot.

By the time I caught up to her, she had just grabbed the handle to her MINI Countryman, but I threw my arm against the door, holding it shut. "Oh, Sophie." I wrapped my arms around her waist and pulled her against my body. "Don't leave so soon."

"Let go of me," she snapped.

Dropping my arms, I took a step back but only gave her enough room to turn and look at me. As if I couldn't help myself, I moved one hand to her hair and wrapped a lock of it around my finger. "Your hair is straight. What happened to all the curls?"

"It changed. Things just happen."

I gave her a quizzical look, I had no clue what that meant. "For years, I was left wondering what the hell happened to you. So many damn nights I stayed awake afraid that I'd go into work the next day only to find out that someone discovered your body. I didn't know if you'd been kidnapped. Raped. I'd waited until you turned eighteen to show you how I felt, to prove to you that my words weren't just words then"—I held my hand out in front of her face and made an explosion gesture—"Poof you were fuckin' gone." Bringing my hands to my face, I slid them down, stretching, trying to erase the emotions that I'm sure she could see. "You know what? Maybe you were just another teenage girl trying to prove that you could get an older guy. It was all just a game to you, wasn't it? Admit it, Sophie." I took a deep breath to regain some control.

She let out a gasp of air at my words. "Please don't be cruel."

"Right, I get it. Like you weren't cruel when you left me broken and confused for ten fucking years. I was an idiot. I believed that I had found my soulmate at twenty, and I believed in love at first sight. Now I know better. I know there's no such thing. It was all just smoke and mirrors. Smoke and fuckin' mirrors." I shoved my hands into my pockets. "If you'll excuse me, you don't have to fake some illness to get away from me, I'll leave instead." I started to turn toward my Jeep, I needed to walk away from Sophia Kostas, close the door on those fucking memories. I wanted to do everything that I could to make her realize that leaving me was the biggest fucking mistake of her life. That was until I saw the tears that had pooled in her eyes, and I couldn't fight the urge to capture one drop as it ran down her cheek. I stepped closer to her then reached out with my finger to let the tear slide toward my palm.

"Don't touch me, don't you dare fucking touch me. You have no clue what I've been through. I owe you an explanation—I admit it, just not tonight. It will take much longer than we have." Her words sounded as if they'd been ripped from her soul.

"I think after what you did to me, right now is the perfect time to explain."

Her eyes narrowed. "You think that you're the only victim here? Let me tell you something, I didn't just break your heart; I broke mine, too. How do you think I felt?" Sophie took a deep breath, as if she were trying to contain the anger and hurt that were clearly visible in her eyes. Only, when she finally managed to shove them away, tears welled against her lashes. "Sometimes it isn't about win or lose, sometimes it's about who's left standing. Guess what? I wasn't left standing."

"I don't get the dramatics. Why are you fucking crying?" I reached for her hands and clenched them in my own. "Princess?" She sucked in a sharp breath at the nickname that I used to call her. "Why are you crying?"

"I don't know, okay. There. I have no clue. I'm just over-whelmed by everything, the change of being back here, you." Her shoulders rising and falling with each deep gasping breath.

"What about me?"

"I don't know. Just you. You aren't nice."

"I'm not nice?"

She shook her head like a child with her lower lip protruding in a pout.

I moved in closer, fully aware that I was being an asshole. "I can show you nice. In fact, I think that I showed you nice on the hood of your car. Remember all the nice things I did to you?" I leaned in and brought my lips next to her ear. "And all the nice things you moaned?" She blushed at my words and the memories I knew that they ignited. "I remember as if it were yesterday. If you only knew the number of times I've dreamed about you. God, I couldn't understand why you left." I brought my forehead to rest against hers.

"I can't believe that all this time you were within reach, you were Kayson's cousin. I searched for you for so long. After you left, I called you and texted you several times a day. Hell, I went by your house every day to look for your car. You know, even after it was sold, I couldn't believe that you weren't coming back."

"Carter, I'm sorry for what I put you through, but I can't do this right now."

"But you can hang out with my sister?"

"I didn't know she was your sister until I saw you two together. I mean, I knew you had a sister, but I didn't know her name and hadn't ever met her. I didn't know you worked with my cousin, either. Yes, we need to clear the air. We need to find a way to get along, and I owe you an explanation. I want to tell you, I do, just now isn't the right time, okay?"

"Sure. Of course. And ten years ago, when you broke my heart that wasn't the right time either. You know what, Soph? I've told myself countless times that I could move on if I only knew why you left. Yet, here you are, and fuck me if I haven't changed my mind. I don't want to hear excuses. It isn't going to change the fact that you left without telling me, cutting me off, and leaving me to wonder what the hell happened to you and what I did wrong."

"Cart—"

"No. Our captain always says, 'Excuses only please the person who is telling them.' I guess I'm just not ready to hear anything that will make you feel better for breaking my damn heart." I shoved my hands through my hair, and Sophie used that moment of freedom to open her car door and jump in. She slammed it shut before I came to my senses, cranking the engine, and leaving me speechless to watch her tail lights disappear out of the parking lot.

Chapter Three
SOPHIE

*S*itting under the porte cochere, I took several deep breaths and replayed what I would say if I saw Carter again. Fuck, I hadn't even noticed if he'd been wearing a wedding ring.

"Hi, Carter. Oh, nice to see you again, Carter. Your wife is so lovely. Oh yes, we met, what was it, ten . . . eleven years ago?"

Yeah right, I sucked as an actress. There was no way I could pretend that Carter and I were nothing more than acquaintances and that I barely remembered him.

Shit. I couldn't do this. Looking down at my chest, I sighed and then glanced out my windshield. I caught sight of a star and made a wish, one that I had made many times.

Twinkle, twinkle, little star, my broken body full of scars.

You gave me strength to fight the fight.

Now give me strength through the night.

With willpower from God knows where, I opened my door and turned, sliding my long legs out of my car before handing my keys over to the valet and taking my claim ticket.

He'd been watching my total freak out for the past ten minutes and probably thought I was drunk since no sane person acted that way. Except me, I did. Well, ever since my run-in with Carter I did.

Looking back to the sky, I searched for my star one more time and then straightened the hem of my shirt, flexed my shoulders, and checked the back of my earrings to make sure that they were secure. Sometimes it was the little things that gave us our inner strength and I was reaching for whatever inner strength I could possibly find.

Walking into the Gaylord Palms Resort, I searched for a sign that directed guests to the ballroom but there wasn't one that I could see, so I followed the hot guys in uniform, which was okay by me.

Unfortunately, the farther we went, the tighter the band around my ribs became. Slowing my pace, I rested my hands on my knees to try and catch my breath. It wasn't from overexertion, no, this was from that feeling of doom that seemed to be slinking in and overtaking me. I wondered if dogs realized that they were getting ready to be euthanized before they were put down. Was this how they felt before they took their final walk? I was fully aware that I was being a drama queen but I had given myself a pass tonight, I was free to have all the irrational thoughts I wanted. But I wasn't free to act irrational so I raced to the first ladies' restroom I could find and yanked the door open then turned and checked to ensure it shut firmly behind me. Resting my hip on the vanity, I tried to force the erratic beating of my heart to calm.

Get your shit together, Sophie, this is not going to get any easier until you come clean. You are going to force him to listen. If not, Carter is going to haunt your every fucking dream. You are going to spend the rest of your life waiting for him to show up everywhere that you go. Time to put on the big girl panties.

Although I had only just mentally decided this, I must've subconsciously decided this earlier today since I was wearing my backless Givenchy blouse. It hid nothing, unlike the shades of ink that crossed my back from my shoulder to my hip in an intricate tattoo. The cherry blossoms wove and dipped below the waistband of my jeans with a spattering of leaves floating in the wind. To most people, it was artwork, but if someone were to get really close, the mask fell away. Then they would see the scars that the tattoo disguised, not that I ever allowed anyone to get that close–ever. My shirt would definitely draw his attention and be a conversation starter.

Leaving the bathroom, I continued on to the ballroom, but my steps were still somewhat hesitant. Once inside, I stopped and admired everything, spinning around and unintentionally imitating Maria from *The Sound of Music* when she came over the mountain singing "The Hills are Alive." This place was alive with thousands of sparkling tiny lights that flickered as chandeliers reflected off rhinestones that Ariel had meticulously placed around the room.

The hairs on the back of my neck prickled, and a weird sense surrounded me. After picking up a flute of champagne from a tray a server was carrying, I took a sip of the bargain bubbly and peered to my left. Standing in the corner with that damn toothy grin was the wannabe toothpaste model himself, Carter. He raised his glass in a salute and drank. I rolled my shoulders and headed toward the bar on the opposite side of the room from him, if I was going to do this, I needed something stronger than what I was currently drinking. On my way to the bar, I spied my cousin Kayson standing with several other officers, I slowly exhaled my breath. The tension in my shoulders relaxed as I neared him.

Damn it all to hell, I need to just go back there and ask Carter to talk. Later, I'll do it later.

I drained my first glass and then grabbed another flute of champagne from a waiter passing by before shifting directions and heading toward Kayson. All the while, I tried to ignore the incredibly handsome man whose eyes were still on me. I knew they were because every tiny fiber of my being was on fire.

Kayson was wearing his official uniform, his shirt neatly starched and his pants tucked into his funky knee-high black leather boots. "Nice boots, I bet you get all the chicks." I leaned up and gave him a peck on the cheek, trying to mask the discomfort that still rumbled in my stomach from Carter.

"Hey, Soph, you look gorgeous. And don't knock the boots, Ariel finds them sexy."

"Let's not go there. Sex, that is one word I never want to hear in the same sentence with you and your fiancée's names. I think that I just vomited in my mouth."

Kayson wrapped an arm around my neck and pulled me in for a brotherly hug. "Want me to tell you about all the ways we get it on?"

"No, no, no. Anything but that." I held my hands out in protest.

He released me as he let out a laugh. "Are you ready for tonight?"

I tried to catch a glimpse of the distant corner of the ballroom to see if Carter was still standing over there, but I couldn't see anything. "Ready to be sold to the highest bidder? Sure, why wouldn't I be? Just promise me that you won't let me go to some sleaze ball."

"Speaking of sleaze balls," he said with a smirk and turned to three guys standing off to our right. "Sophie, meet Aiden, Max, and Eli. I'll make sure they don't bid on you."

"Nice to meet you guys." I nodded. Instantly figuring out that Kayson was joking as the guys were cutting up with him over his snide remark. Aiden and Max wore the same uniform as Kayson and Carter, clearly marking them as motorcycle deputies.

Aiden leaned in and gave me a hug. "No worries, I plan on bidding on you."

"I hope that you brought a lot of money." Eli smacked Aiden's shoulder. "Most of the single guys at the station want to bid on Sophie just to piss Kayson off. You know how protective these Greeks are with their female family members."

I couldn't hold back my smile. These guys obviously knew my cousin well and enjoyed torturing him.

"Oh, here's someone else I want you to meet." Kayson interrupted us. "Carter, this is Sophie. Sophie, I'd like you to meet one of my closest friends, Carter. I think you know his sister Stella."

Doing two things at once was easy when those two things were rolling your eyes and biting your tongue, which was exactly what I was doing as I turned to face Carter. Really? Why couldn't he just stay in his damn corner?

"Nice to meet you." Carter took my hand in his and gave it a light squeeze as if this were the first time we'd met. "So, Sophie, tell us about yourself. Married?" Carter kept my hand clutched in his.

"Nope . . ." I tried to shake my hand loose.

"Children?"

"No, I've—" I yanked back, pulling my hand free but almost losing my balance in the process.

"What do you do?"

"I'm an author, I write—"

"Kayson mentioned that you used to live here? How long are you back for?"

Fuck, Carter wasn't giving me a chance to finish a

sentence. Glancing at Kayson, I silently pleaded with him to rescue me.

"Your glass is empty," Kayson said as he reached for the flute and let out a cough, darting his eyes between Carter and me. "What can I get you?"

"A Riesling if they have it. If not, then any white wine will do."

I watched Kayson, hoping that Carter would take the hint and leave, but he didn't. Instead, he grabbed my shoulders and spun me back to face him. I met Carter's fury and heard his anger etched in every word. "Where the fuck is the rest of your shirt?"

Heat rose up the back of my neck, and for some fucking reason the air conditioner in the room must have stopped working because I was sweating. "Get your hands off me. Last time I checked, you weren't my father and I was a grown woman."

"Funny, last time I checked, you had just turned eighteen, oh, and then you fucking disappeared."

Ariel's voice interrupted us. "If I could get all auction participants to come to the front of the stage please."

"Tell Kayson to save my drink for me," I snapped at him, then turned and headed to the stage to slip behind a curtain where Ariel was waiting. She was standing with a man and three women, one of whom was dressed as a fabulous rendition of Whitney Houston.

"Let me introduce everyone," Ariel said as she walked over and wove her fingers through mine, giving me a reassuring squeeze. "This is Ringo, our opening act who will be singing 'One Moment in Time' by Whitney, of course."

We all replied, "Of course."

"When he begins . . ."

I turned to look at the man across from me as he let out a

cough, and I smiled at the realization that he hadn't known Whitney was a drag queen impersonator.

"Y'all will come up to the stage one at a time. When the first person gets to the center mark, the next person will begin their ascent. I have three officers to escort each of the ladies to their position on the stage, Lorenzo you'll walk alone, and I want you right there." Ariel pointed to a spot directly under a chandelier. "Now, let me introduce y'all to each other. This is Sophia Christakos, she's the New York Times bestselling author of the children's series *History Hunter*. We have Pandora Robicheaux"—Ariel pointed to a svelte woman with great bone structure who reminded me of one of the Olson twins— "she's a model for *Throttle* magazine as well as a columnist."

"Hi, everyone," Pandora said, offering up a small wave.

"This is Lorenzo Pavese." Holy shit, I'd finally gotten a good look at the man and if I were ever asked to describe bedroom eyes, it would be his. He was all Italian, olive skin, lush ebony hair, and dark eyes that bore into mine. He raised one corner of his mouth in a smirk and then bent to drop a kiss on the top of my hand. "He's the founder and CEO of Duchessa Cruise Lines. Last, but certainly not least, is Juliet Lovehart." I was taken aback by what sounded like an obviously fake name. She was the one that was height challenged in our group. I was tall, Pandora was in heels that put her close to my height, and Lorenzo was well over six feet. Juliet looked positively tiny standing next to us. "She is the host of the syndicated radio show Dear Juliet," Ariel said as she finished our introductions.

"Wow, great name." And for a relationship talk show, it truly was.

"It is, would you believe me if I told you that it's my real name, as in given to me at birth?" Juliet asked.

"Not for one second," I replied, letting out a laugh.

"It is. My mom loved our last name so much and was such a romantic that she named me Juliet."

"Don't tell me, you have a brother named Romeo?"

"No." Juliet paused for a second. "Darcy."

"No fucking way." Pandora joined in.

"Yes, fucking way."

I smiled at Juliet's reply and how out of place it sounded coming from her.

"I'm going to go play host." Ariel gave us all a wide smile. "Ringo are you ready?"

"Darling this ass was born ready. Now, you go be fabulous." Ariel walked off, and Ringo lowered his voice. "Any chance you can be persuaded to swing for my team?" Lorenzo jumped back at Ringo's question. "Just kiddin', doll face. I can smell a breeder a mile away. Now, the real question is can any of these fine men in uniform be lured to bat for the other team?"

Pandora, Juliet, and I held on to each other as we tried to hold back our laughter. The looks crossing Lorenzo's face as Ringo continued his one-man—or was that one-woman, rather—discussion was hysterical. Ringo obviously went for the shock factor.

I turned to the other ladies just as the crowd fell silent to listen to Ariel make the requisite thank yous and then signal for Ringo. He climbed the stairs, the music began, and when he opened his mouth, I thought I had died and gone to Heaven.

"Is that him singing?" Juliet asked our small group.

"Yeah, I think it is, but more importantly, I think it's our signal to start. You're up, Juliet."

I was the last of the women, thank God. There was something to say about having an S as your first initial. Ariel had lined us up in alphabetical order according to our first name.

Staring up at the stage, I watched as Juliet was met by a

man in uniform, he held out his arm and escorted her to the designated spot before twirling her and striding off the stage. As Pandora and her escort inched closer to her mark my heart picked up speed.

I prided myself on being the type of person to never give into theatrics. I guess that it was no big shocker that if I was ever going to change that stance, tonight was it. Images of Anne Boleyn and Marie Antoinette facing the guillotine filled my head. Okay, I know that it wasn't exactly the same thing but just like that damn dog taking his last walk to be euthanized this seemed to be my night of doom.

When it was finally my turn, I stared up and into the green eyes of a handsome man in uniform as he held out his arm and said, "Smile darling, everyone's watching." My tension eased at his words. "That's it love, now let out a little laugh like I just told you the funniest thing in the entire world, and you will have them eating out of the palms of your hands."

I couldn't help it, I laughed at his words. When I reached my spot, I reached up and gave him a peck on his cheek. "Thank you." He was genuinely one of the nice ones.

He winked.

The auction began, and I wasn't sure what to expect. Officers worked hard, but they didn't make a ton of money. That didn't stop Ringo from walking around the stage and adding humor to raise the bids. The four of us along with the silent auction in another room would help families of fallen deputies.

Once Juliet and Pandora's auctions were complete, I relaxed a little, both of them ended close to five hundred dollars, which was great considering it was only for a dinner partner and a dance. Ariel called my name and opened the bidding at fifty dollars.

A voice to my left shouted, "Fifty." I couldn't see the face because the lights on stage were bright and blinding. From the same area, another voice countered the bid, "Sixty." In a deepening growl, the first bidder raised his offer, but then a third voice joined in, taking the bid higher. Once again, the original bidder stayed in and fought.

Ariel stepped back from the mic and allowed the three men to duke it out. The crowd enjoyed the show as bidders two and three increased their bids by small increments, taking turns outbidding the first bidder. If only the crowd would shut the hell up, I might be able to hear the voices better. I doubted one of the guys was Carter. He was too angry to waste his money on me. Plus, the guys earlier had said that people wanted to bid just to aggravate Kayson, this was all just to torture him, it was all in good fun, I silently reminded myself.

It still didn't stop me from squinting out into the crowd to try and see a face. Lorenzo had scooted next to me and in a soft whisper said, "Someone wants you very bad, and his friends aren't making it easy for him. From what I can see, they are making him work for you. Never fear, pet, you are the belle of the ball."

Lorenzo returned to his position as the bid hit five hundred dollars. Hoping this debacle was almost over, I let out a sigh and then froze when one last shout boomed from the first bidder. "Seven hundred fifty dollars." And it was at that moment that I was one hundred percent sure that I knew that voice.

Ariel waited to see if anyone countered, but when no one said anything, she took a step up to the mic. "Do I hear seven sixty?" She waited. "No? Okay, seven fifty going once, twice, we have a winner, a very tenacious winner."

The crowd applauded and then separated to make room for the winner to fetch his prize. In my mind, I wanted this moment to be like *An Officer and A Gentleman* when Richard

Gere strode in and all the factory workers separated so he could sweep Debra Winger off her feet. Instead, this was more like the movie *Babe,* and I was the piglet being won at the county fair and everyone was applauding the victor. Carter came into view, a look of pure satisfaction and determination smoldering on his face.

*H*olding out my hand to help Sophie down the stairs, I felt her shaking, and my anger from the other night at Sixes seemed to fade away and all I saw was my Sophie.

She put on her best frigid bitch face, trying to hide all her emotions. "Carter, I'm glad to see you. Where's your date?" Really? I just bid on her and won, and she thinks I came with a date? I raised one brow in an attempt to encourage her to rethink her question.

"Right. . .well. . ." She cleared her throat and started over. "Anyway, it's nice to see you again. I guess that we'll find each other before dinner, huh?" She moved to take a step away, but I wrapped her in the fold on my arm before she could. My fingers brushed against the exposed skin of her open-back blouse as I escorted her over to the corner. Caging her in, our eyes locked, and she tried to defuse our situation with humor. "You know, you're crazy for spending seven hundred fifty dollars, you way overpaid. There was probably a coupon online, maybe you can ask for a friend's discount." She tried to slide out from my arms, but I moved my hands to her waist and held her in place. "Why did you bid on me? If you're wanting an apology? You could have saved your money." I stared down at her hand that she had just moved up and placed on my chest, and she kept talking not realizing what she had done. "I won't apologize for doing what I thought was best for me ten years ago. The only thing I have to apologize for is hurting you, Carter. So, I'm sorry that happened. I really am. It wasn't my intention to hurt you or upset you. And if there is anything I can do to make this right, all you have to do is tell me, and it's done. Just remember that sometimes we have to accept that things happen, and when they do, we have three choices: fight, give up, or change our direction." She slipped out from between the wall and me and took a single step before I grabbed her elbow gently.

"Can I talk now?" I asked softly, watching as she bit her bottom lip and nodded sheepishly. My heart clenched as memories flooded me as I remembered the nights she'd sit in my cruiser and I'd grip the steering wheel, my knuckles turning white as I fought back my urge to run my hands over her body. Just the hint of her perfume had me all kinds of twisted when we were young. "I don't want to fight. I didn't bid on you just so I could hear some apology, I bid on you to start over. I want to get to know you. Let's go join the others. I think it's time for us to go into the dining area anyway. We can call a truce for one evening."

"Really?"

"Yes, really."

Thoughtfully, she caught her bottom lip between her teeth again before releasing it to say, "I think I can handle that."

This time when she turned to leave, I didn't stop her. Instead, I walked next to her, my hand on the small of her back as we moved toward the main ballroom where a dance floor was set up with a DJ in the corner. Banquet tables were placed in a U-shape five rows deep to seat at least five hundred people. Nestled against the far perimeter of the wall were tables for two, each set up with flowers, candlelight, and a place card stating that the table was reserved.

"I'm assuming one of those is ours?"

"Yeah. Ariel said the back wall." Sophie pointed in that direction.

Weaving through couples that stopped us to introduce themselves to Sophia the famous author or congratulate me on the winning bid seemed to take forever, but eventually we found our table. We sat quietly for a few moments staring at each other, I was taking her in, trying to catalogue the differences in her from then and now.

That's when I realized poets were liars, silence wasn't golden—it was lonely. I had been lonely for ten years, not allowing anyone to get close. And there she was, the girl who had taken the title of The One Who Got Away. I wouldn't waste another second being angry, at least not tonight. I wanted to know everything about her, what made her smile, if she still listened to Avril . . .

"Do you remember that time I pulled you over, and when I got to your car you blamed speeding on a song?" Her face illuminated as she remembered that moment. "When I asked who Avril was, you nearly lost it."

"You don't know Avril?" Sophie grinned, delivering the same line from all those years ago. "I was offended, how did anyone not know who she was. I wanted to name my child Avril."

"As in Lavigne?" I asked, following her lead through our past conversation.

"Oh my God, you do know her. You were totally redeemed

with that acknowledgment. I was speeding because of her song 'Girlfriend.' I was at the part where she sang about being a motherfucking princess, and I was playing air drums on my gas pedal."

"I let you off with a warning because you were a motherfucking princess." I let out a low chuckle. "I think that was the last night I pulled you over for speeding and not just to talk. God, you were so young."

"Hey, sometimes I saw you first and pulled up to you," Sophie corrected me.

I picked up my glass of water and took a long swallow as a waiter set our salads in front of us and a basket of warm rolls between. It was like a fucking Hallmark movie or one of those butter commercials where our hands touched as we passed the rolls. Whatever it was, my dick liked it, and he was fully aware that the woman of our dreams, who was drop-dead gorgeous—was sitting across from us.

"What's life like as an author? Do you have set hours or days that you work?" I made small talk as we ate our salad.

"Not really set hours, meaning I can take off whenever I want. But I'm pretty disciplined, I try to be in my office every morning by nine. I work it as if it were any other nine-to-five job."

"Does it get lonely?"

"You mean, do I get tired of not having to answer to anyone else, having bitchy coworkers, or having to share breakrooms and bathrooms?"

"Okay, I see what you mean. You obviously like working alone." Sophie was slowly relaxing, which was exactly what I wanted to see. "Kayson said that you were moving back but not to where? Did you get all settled?"

A smile spread across her lips, and she radiated happiness. "Yes. I live around the corner from him." She clearly loved her family.

"What is it with Greeks and their houses? Kayson and his brothers all got a house."

"A lot of Mediterranean cultures do it, sometimes they will pool money to buy newlyweds a house, but if someone in particular can do it—in this case it was Uncle George since he builds homes for a living—then it usually falls on that person. It's our way of keeping our family close and secure."

"Oh, you're a newlywed?" I cringed at the thought of Sophie being married.

"No. My family is just nuts. Or maybe I should say imposing, it's their way of making us feel guilty so we don't leave. You know, giving us roots."

As she finished and set her fork down, I did the same. The server cleared our salad plates and placed our dinners in front of us. The metallic ting of silverware on china roared in the hollow cocoon surrounding the two of us.

I couldn't help but smile and give a quiet thank you to Kayson's dad. We fell silent as we ate our entrée. When those plates were cleared, our waiter set our desserts in front of us, cheesecake. He held one of those server things with three bowls, and Sophie smiled brightly. "Would you care for cherries, strawberries, or blueberries for the top of your cheesecake?" he asked.

"Blueberries." Sophie and I both said in unison.

He drizzled the fruit on top and walked to the next table.

"Why are you smiling?"

"You know that dish he was carrying?"

I nodded at her question.

"Do you know what it's called?"

I shook my head.

"It's called an olive branch dish because of the way the bowls shoot off from each other like an olive stem."

"Should we take it as a sign and extend an olive branch?"

"I'd like that. We can give that to each other for this one night, can't we?"

"Yeah." What I didn't say was what I really wanted was for her to give me one real night. Let me know what one night would have been like with Sophie in my arms, the one night we should have had if she had stayed. But I didn't mention that, of course not, I kept that to myself.

"ou two ready? Opening dance is in five minutes," Ariel said as she placed a hand on my back and then moved on to the next table before we answered.

Taking one last sip of water before being forced to face my fears of being in Carter's arms and losing my heart, I wiped my mouth and then stood. I turned to the sound of chatter from Lorenzo, Pandora, and Juliet plus their winning dates.

"Showtime," Pandora said.

"You okay, pet?" Lorenzo asked almost intimately, whispering against my ear. "You don't look as if you're having fun."

"I'm fine, just tired." Carter was next to me, and I hadn't known that his arm could hold me any tighter until that moment when he squeezed me closer to him, effectively moving me a few inches away from Lorenzo.

The first notes strummed through the air as we walked on to the floor to Enrique Iglesias's "Hero," which was the perfect song in so many ways. Deputies were heroes and put their lives on the line every day.

Carter kept his right hand around my waist and spun me into his chest, sliding his left hand up to cup my face. I was afraid to meet his eyes, scared that I would see everything I was feeling mirrored back in his icy blue depths.

I couldn't breathe, my head spun, my heart tightened as if it were going to stop beating at any moment. I had no clue how I'd go on after tonight, once this dinner and dance were over and Carter and I went our separate ways, he'd return to whoever warmed his bed and I'd return to my solitary life.

I jerked up at the sound of Carter's voice as he sang the words to the song. He was as lost in his own thoughts as I had just been—I didn't think he even realized that he was singing out loud.

The song ended, and the DJ opened the floor to everyone else. When the next song began, I knew it was time that I broke the gloominess that surrounded us.

"How long have you been with Orange County?"

"Eight years."

"Do you like being in motors?"

"I love it. I don't think I'd like going back to driving around in a cage car. Plus, I used to like my sergeant." Carter pointed to Kayson, who'd come up behind me just as one song ended and another began. Fully aware that Kayson overheard him.

"We'll talk later," Kayson said teasing Carter in return. "Care if I cut in?" Carter stepped back then swooped Ariel into an exaggerated spin as my cousin took his place in front of me.

"So, what's up? You okay?" Kayson asked. "You look so intense tonight."

"Oh God, yes. I'm just overwhelmed. Ariel really did a stellar job. This place is beautiful."

Kayson's hand lifted my chin and forced me to give him my full attention.

"Yeah, not buying it but kudos for trying to divert the topic. Are you mad that Carter won the bid? He's a good guy, you don't need to worry about him."

"Yeah, he seems like a decent guy," I said as casually as I could. "I'm not mad at all, I promise."

"Well, I'm glad you're here. You were gone a long time, Sophie, and you missed out on a lot. There are a ton of people I want you to meet."

He was right, ten years was a long time and while I had been suffering in California, I had left a lot of people suffering back here. We twirled around in silence after that, his piercing brown eyes, the same as mine, trying to intimidate me into telling him something.

"What happened? Why did you leave and cut us out of your life?"

"I'm just not ready to talk yet. Truthfully, I need to talk with Carter first."

"Carter? Why would you need to talk with Carter first, we're your family? You know that my pop is only going to give you so much time before he is knocking down your front door, right?" Kayson's voice was a mix of concern and anger at being left out.

"Yeah, I know. I promise, soon."

The song ended, and I leaned up and kissed Kayson on the cheek. "I promise, I will explain everything, I'll make everything right."

Satisfied with my answer for now, Kayson released my hand, and Carter cut back in, wrapping me in his arms to keep anyone else from cutting in.

"Did you have fun dancing with Ariel?"

"She's as bad as my sister."

Carter placed both of his hands on my hips and pulled me against him as we swayed to the music.

"How is that?" I didn't see any similarities between Stella and Ariel.

"She believes that I'm hiding something from her, and she's determined to figure it out."

"Like what? What does she think you're hiding?" A fluttering in my stomach had me leaning into him so I didn't have to meet his eyes just in case he said that Ariel was suspicious of us. I had tried so hard to hide my feelings.

Carter didn't answer me at first. Instead, he slid his hands from my waist so that he could slide his fingers up my neck and through my hair.

"Sophie, tell me I'm not the only crazy one? We were kids when we met, right?"

My heart raced, but I nodded at Carter's whispered words that seemed like a weird question. "No, you're not crazy."

"Why haven't I gotten over you? Jesus Christ, I mean, we fooled around, but we didn't even . . ."

One of his large hands moved back to my waist, as if he was going to dip me in front of everyone.

"Did you mean it when you said you would do anything to make this right between us?" His voice was a cross between a purr and a growl, it was seductive.

"I did."

"Well, I know what it is, it's what I need, what I've always needed."

"What?" Goose bumps trailed along my arms, and a little tremor quivered in my voice.

"I need our one night. I need to know you in every way possible. I've needed it for ten years."

I froze at his words, stopped swaying to the rhythm of the song, and took a step back. Holy fuck. That? Of all the things . . . that is what he asked for? Could I give him that and still walk away, let him be with other women? He deserved someone else. Carter Lang was a good man. He would make an amazing father and an even greater husband . . . for someone, not me.

"Sophia."

I glanced up, meeting his eyes again at his use of my real name, no nickname.

"Princess, I need this, I want this. I've wanted you, dreamed of you for ten years." He pulled me back in, holding me flush against him, and his thick hard shaft was rigid and pressing against me, proof that he definitely wanted me. "What do you want?"

That was a loaded question, what did I want? I wanted to be eighteen again and have a different life. I wanted a night with him. I wanted to be a wife, a mom, a lover . . . his lover.

"I want you, one night." But how could I keep him from seeing? Curling my shoulders forward, I caught myself going into my natural protective mode. It's what took the focus off my chest and put it more on the rest of my body. It was as close to a ball that I could make myself.

"Soph, look at me. Are you sure?"

I nodded. I could do one night. I walked away once, I could do it again, right?

He bent and lightly nibbled on my ear. "I have a room."

My body uncurled and extended as shivers raced down my spine and every hair raised. I was on the verge of losing control. I had to remind myself of things that normally came naturally. Breathe in, breathe out, deep breaths. I kept telling myself that I could do this, I could so do this.

Carter's soft tug on my hand had me following him out of the ballroom and to the bank of elevators. We walked in and the doors closed. Watching as he pressed number seven, then a second later, the doors slid open. The whole way up neither of us said anything, and I spent the time wondering just how horrible and stupid of a decision this was. He opened his hotel room door and held it while I walked under his arm. Before the door slammed shut, his hands were on my hips, and he turned me to face him. This was it, the moment of truth, the failsafe line.

"Carter." His name escaped my lips in a drawn-out, raspy breath. I drank in his woodsy scent as he urged me deeper into the room. When the backs of my legs hit the mattress, I collapsed onto the edge of the bed as he dropped to his knees in front of me. Captivated, I sank into the feel of his fingers lightly scratching his way up my thighs. His calloused hands tickled as he trailed along my skin. He continued his upward movement until he reached my face and cupped my cheeks. I didn't dare blink and risk missing a single moment.

"Sophie, you have no clue how much I've thought about you. You're here, and you're so fucking beautiful." He leaned in and pressed his lips to the curve of my neck, and then with tiny kisses, he traced his way up to my ear and back around to my lips. His kiss was soft at first, almost as if he were asking me for permission. He tasted of sugar and blueberries and Carter, just this overwhelming taste of everything that was wonderful in the world. I leaned into him just a bit, and the slide of his tongue against mine was everything I remembered it to be. The tingling sensations made my toes curl when our tongues twirled and danced. Moving his hands down and over my body, the heat radiated through my clothes but when his fingers crossed my bare back, it was a fire pressing me tightly against him.

"Carter, I never forgot about you," I whispered against his lips, relishing in the way his lips smiled against mine before he deepened the kiss again.

When he released his hold, and slid his hands from my back to the hem of my shirt, panic flooded me, and I shoved his hands away. I tried to right my overreaction by glancing down and concentrating on steadying my hands while I unbuttoned his uniform shirt. I hadn't even noticed that he'd already removed his boots until he stood, bringing me up with him. His fingers moved to my jeans and I mimicked his movements, unsnapping his pants. Wrapping my fingers into his waistband, it hit me, I was touching Carter. My God. I yanked his shirt free and slid my fingers across his skin before I lowered his pants and took in the sight. He was wearing black boxer briefs, which left no room to my imagination.

Carter returned the gesture, slipping my jeans off and helping me step out of them as I unfastened my necklace and earrings.

Breaking away, I stuffed my jewelry in my purse and took a deep breath before I returned to him. He was sitting on the bed and had removed his shirt, I crawled up the bed with the first inklings of doubt slowly creeping in.

He leaned forward and cupped me under my chin, pulling my lips to his. My fingers grazed his perfect abs, their tightly sculpted muscles flexing as I slowly worked down to brush my hand across his hard, throbbing erection. I took a deep swallow, my mind filled with images. He was much more defined than when we were young, all the lingering traces of boy were gone.

Curving my hand to rest around the imprint of his cock, I squeezed and he pulsated beneath my touch. It sent a thrill through me that I controlled him at that moment . . . well, until his fingers wrapped around my arm and pulled me down. He rolled on top of me, pressing me into the billowy covers. Straddling my legs, he braced himself over me and peered down, and I couldn't help but notice the wet mark on the front of his boxers. That mark might as well have been a bucket of water at that moment because everything right down to my marrow froze. If we went any further, he'd want my shirt off, and his words, "I'm not ready to hear excuses," echoed in my brain. With jerky movements, I shook my head and pressed my palms to his chest.

"Carter, I'm sorry—" He slid off me and threw himself onto the bed.

"Don't. Let's not go there tonight, okay?"

I raised my head and looked in his eyes, seeing ten years' worth of hurt he had kept buried deep reflecting all the dreams I had secretly stored away. It was that one look that sealed the deal—or rather, unsealed the deal—for us. I couldn't stay. "I'm sorry, Carter, I can't. I can't be a one-night stand." I crawled off the bed and ran over to put my jeans on before picking up my shoes and slinging my purse over my shoulder.

"Wait, Sophie. We don't have to do anything. I just want to get to know you."

"No, you don't. You want your one night. It's a ten-year-old debt, and you came tonight to collect. I get it, I do. But you won't let me explain. You want to pick and choose which parts of me that you want to know." Opening the door, I raced out into the hall, his voice calling my name trailing behind me all the way to the elevator.

Repeatedly, my thumb smashed against the button, impatient. Okay, I knew it wasn't going to bring the elevator faster, but it sure as fuck made me feel better. I expected to see him any moment, but he didn't appear. When the elevator dinged, I let out a sigh of relief. Stepping in, I pressed lobby and then slipped my shoes on while the elevator descended. I thought about what had almost happened. God, I had been so stupid to think I would have been able to go through with it. I was still berating myself as I stepped off the elevator and headed to the double doors that led outside and handed the valet my ticket.

While I waited, I moved to the shadows just in case

Carter decided to come out and look for me and pulled out a few bills to tip the valet. When my car pulled to a stop at the curb, I traded the cash for my keys and slid behind the wheel.

Carter Lang didn't chase.

~

I THREW a pillow over my head and burrowed deeper into my covers, trying to ignore whoever was leaning on my doorbell. When the intruder to my sleep didn't go away and added knocking to the god-awful ringing, I snagged my phone to check the time. It was almost ten in the morning. Fuck, I hadn't slept this late since, well . . . it had been years. Tossing back the covers, I got out of bed and slowly walked downstairs, prepared to give whichever one of my family members woke me a verbal lashing.

Unfortunately, when I swung the door open, I was face to face with Carter. He lowered his aviators and lifted his lips into a smirk. "Morning, sunshine. I brought Krispy Kreme." He held out the box of heavenly sent goodness, which I ripped from his hands before turning to slam the door in his face. I was absolutely ready to eat the entire dozen glaze-smothered, light, and fluffy donuts myself. But my door didn't latch because asshole had his foot in the way.

"Mind moving your shoe?" I opened the box and pulled out a donut, which was still warm, and took a bite before mumbling, "I didn't ask for the wake-up call."

"Are you always so grumpy in the morning?"

"Mm-hmm, when I have uninvited guests that don't text first, yes." I took another bite and headed to my kitchen to make coffee. I looked at him as he dropped his keys and sunglasses on my counter and settled onto a barstool. "I guess this means you're staying. Just know that the first cup is mine." I grabbed a K-cup and tossed it into the Keurig before

I stuffed the rest of the donut into my mouth and moved to the fridge to grab the creamer. Catching my reflection in the glass of my microwave almost made me cringe. My hair was sticking up in several different directions, and I wasn't dressed. Well, I was, but it was my pajamas. I hadn't removed last night's makeup either, so it was smeared in dark smudges under my eyes.

Pulling back my shoulders, I turned to face him, he was right fucking behind me. "What do you want? Oh wait, let me go grab my purse, and I'll write you a check to reimburse you for the seven hundred fifty dollars that you're out."

"Stop it, Soph, fucking stop this, will you? I want to talk to you. I went to that auction for one reason."

"I know, you told me, but I can't give it to you. I can't do one-night stands."

"If you really think that's all I'm after, you need to re-evaluate things. I haven't been able to get you out of my mind. There is something between us, and you can't tell me that you didn't feel it last night. I'm not asking for anything definite. I'm just asking you to give me a chance. Let's go out. Let's spend some time together. We may find out that we still have the same feelings that we did ten years ago."

"And you may find out that I'm not the same person I was ten years ago. You have no fucking clue who I was back then. Hell, I had no clue. I was a naïve teenager and thought that I was a motherfucking princess, you were Prince Charming, and we were going to live happily fucking ever after." I turned to add Stevia and cream to my coffee then put a fresh K-cup in the maker for Carter before grabbing my cup and heading for my room.

"If you're a motherfucking princess, then I'm going to Prince Charm the fuck out of you," he hollered after me as I moved to my stairs.

I let out a laugh. "I'm going to go change. Make yourself

at home. I'll be right back." If he only knew. I was more like Harry Fucking Houdini than I was a princess. I didn't think anyone's dreams could disappear quicker than mine had. I was restrained and drowning, and there was no key and no way to escape.

Chapter Six

CARTER

*H*olding my cup of coffee, I thought about my plan of attack. She may be different, but so was I, we both had lived two separate lives. We had pasts that neither of us knew about, but I could accept that. I just needed to keep reminding myself that I had her now.

When she walked back into the kitchen twenty minutes later, her dark hair was damp and pinned back, which made her even more breathtaking.

"What are you doing today?"

She paused, considering my question before saying, "Nothing. Why?"

"Well, I volunteer at the community center and was on my way there when I stopped by. I'd love it if you came with me, and I'm sure the kids would enjoy it as well. When I learned who you were and that you wrote children's books, I asked some of the kids if they'd read your work. They all thought I was nuts, and two of the kids pulled copies of your books from their backpacks. So, you may get some hero worship."

She grabbed another donut from the box and took a bite.

"I have a few boxes of books that I was going to donate to a local school. Would the center like them instead?"

"They'd love them. Does that mean you're going to come with me? I took this week off because this is Orange County's spring break and the center will be packed."

She shoved the rest of the donut in her mouth. "Let me get this straight. You schedule your vacation for when kids are out of school so that you can volunteer at a center and spend time with them?"

"Pretty much, but only one week. I get more vacation than that."

"But still. And why aren't you married with children?"

Because you never gave me my heart back.

I went with the safer reply instead. "I could ask you the same thing."

The instant I said it, I regretted my words because something in her changed.

"Touché."

I followed Sophie out of her massive great room area and down a hallway. We passed two rooms—one filled with boxes and a bathroom. Ahead, behind an intricately carved door, was her office.

"A round room. That's different."

"It's called a turret. Victorian-style home and all that. Would you mind carrying those out to your car?" Sophie gestured to two boxes sitting by her desk.

"Sure. Be right back."

As I headed out, I paid closer attention to her home. The living room and kitchen were one giant area that was divided by a bar. On the other side of the kitchen was another one of those turrets, which seemed to be her dining room. Behind me were giant French doors that opened to a lanai and in front of me was her foyer and front door.

Heading outside I loaded the boxes into the back of my

Jeep and then closed the tailgate. Before going back in, I looked around and tried to picture what was upstairs, letting my eyes track along the front of the two-story home. That was when it hit me—this was a family home.

"Earth to Carter, come in Carter." Sophie's voice had a soft lull to it, a lightness that didn't seem to be there last night.

I smiled at her. Sophie was carrying a book bag, and when I took it from her, she met me with a smile equally as bright as the sun shining this morning. I held out my hand and escorted her to the passenger side of my Jeep.

"Is this okay to wear?" She did a little spin, letting the long flowy skirt of her dress billow out around her.

"You look beautiful. What's in the bag?"

"Just some stuff I might need if I decide to volunteer as well. You never know."

"You never know." It was hard to contain my smile. I opened her door, helped her up, and waited while she pulled in the edges of her skirt. Once she was in, I moved to the driver's side, and we were on our way over to the community center.

"What have you been up to? Tell me about your job, what got you into writing children's books?"

"Well, I got started because I love kids and history, so it seemed like such an organic way to put the things that I enjoyed together."

"So, you write about history? I hated history when I was a kid."

I watched as her face lit up, and she radiated with excitement. "That's what makes my job so interesting, trying to write in a way that will make kids *want* to read. My series, the one that most people know"— she twisted in her seat and tucked one leg up under her, practically bouncing—"is about a little boy who wants to be an archeologist when he grows up so wherever he goes, he digs in the dirt."

"Is this History Hunter?"

"Yup!" She beams. "Well, when he is in Gettysburg, he finds an Indian head penny from 1863, which is the same year that Abraham Lincoln gave his famous address. That penny takes him back in time to November 19, 1863, to witness the events of that day. And, when he is in Boston, he finds a china cup, which takes him back to what leads to the Boston Tea Party. Every book is a different story."

"You really enjoy writing and researching, don't you?"

"Oh my God, I love it. I love going into the schools and reading chapters or helping kids who want to be writers one day. My favorite part is when a child tells me that they hate history, I read them part of a story, and they don't realize that those things really happened. They are so enthralled in the story, they have no clue that they are learning history at the same time."

Watching her and the excitement she had over making an impact on a child's life I knew that Sophie was going to be a fabulous mom one day. An image wrapped around my brain of Sophie carrying a baby in her arms. Fuck, just the thought of her having a baby with some man—any other man—made my blood boil. She was mine. She had been since that first day our eyes locked. I couldn't think about that, so instead, I focused on the fact that she was sitting next to me.

Pulling into the parking lot, I smiled when I saw some of my favorite kids on the other side of the fence. I knew I shouldn't have favorites, but it was hard not to.

"Come on, let's get you introduced." I got out and walked around to open Sophie's door before grabbing the boxes from the back. The two of us headed inside, and I set the books on a table. "This is the library and homework area. You can come back later to unpack those and put them wherever you want or I can take care of it this week."

"Thank goodness you're here, Carter, these kids have too much energy." The director of the center was standing in the doorway, looking a bit flustered.

I smiled. "It's Sunday, what did you expect? No kid wants to be here on a Sunday," I said, giving her a wide smile. "Denise, I want you to meet someone, I have a new volunteer for you."

"You're an angel, has anyone ever told you that?" Denise placed a kiss on my cheek. She was the same age as my mom, and her son, Logan, was a firefighter who volunteered here as well.

"Denise, this is Sophia Kostas. She's the author of those books that I was asking the kids about."

"It's so nice to meet you." Denise grabbed Sophie and pulled her in for a hug. To her credit, Sophie hugged her back. Denise could be overwhelming sometimes, but she was a miracle worker when it came to the center and helping these kids. "Why don't you come with me, and we can get some paperwork filled out. I will have to run a background check and do fingerprints. It's just standard protocol."

"No worries." Sophie reached into her book bag and pulled out a sealed envelope and a file folder before handing both to Denise. "Here's a certified sealed copy of my background check, a copy of my resume, references, and personal information so you can verify everything. I'm already in the system. I do a lot of school visits, so I totally understand protocol. You'll also find a copy of my insurance with rider that covers me with children when I'm in my author capacity."

"You just became my very best friend." Denise wrapped an arm around Sophie again before stopping and looking back at me. "Why are you still standing here? Kids need to be run ragged."

Taking that as my cue to go, I headed outside and spotted the cutest of all the kids laying on the grass staring up at the sky. Again, I knew I wasn't supposed to have favorites, but if I ever had children, I wanted one that looked just like Bee. I wasn't sure if that was her real name or not but that's what her mom called her, and it somehow seemed to fit. Not only was she adorable but she was smart and thought about things that the average kid didn't even consider.

I came in and sat next to her, stretching out and then lying back to stare up at the vast amount of clouds.

"What do you see today?" I asked knowing that this was her favorite thing to do when she was at the center.

She pointed off to the left where three clouds connected with smaller clouds. "That's a family. The tiny cloud in the center, that's the child, the mom and dad are on either side."

"Any particular family?"

"Nope, just a family."

Her reply was quick, but it didn't sound as if she was hurt or missing something in her life. Bee's mom was a single parent. I wasn't sure if her dad was in the picture at all and it wasn't my position to ask. "Tell me, what else do you see?"

"See that long cloud?"

"Yep."

"That's a caterpillar. It's almost to those big clouds. When they moosh together, that will be when she breaks free and becomes a butterfly."

"You know what I see?" I pointed to the right toward a perfectly shaped cumulus cloud.

"What?" Bee asked enthusiastically.

"See that puffy one over there? That's a bumble bee, and she is floating around to all of the other clouds and making them happy. Just like you."

"Do I make people happy?"

"You make me happy whenever I see you. I can't help but smile. And every time I see your mom, she's smiling. Seems like when you're around people are happy."

"Thanks, Carter."

"I'm headed out to the field," I said as I stood up. "If you want to come join us for a game you're welcome."

"Nah, I'd rather stay here and dream."

Leaving Bee to her clouds and her imagination, I raced off. When I got to the middle of the field, I blew my whistle to get the kids' attention. They came running, and Logan came barreling down the stairs at the sound of my whistle as well.

"Want to get a game going?" he asked.

"Sure. The usual?" When the kids had too much energy, our go-to game was soccer. Nothing exhausted them more than running up and down a field.

"Let's line up and begin with some stretches." The kids formed a haphazard line in front of Logan and me and mimicked my motions as I lead them through the first few sets of stretches.

"Did you get a look at the new volunteer? I'm calling dibs," Logan whispered while the kids were busy touching their toes.

"Keep away."

"Hey, I called her first."

Letting out a low snort. "Don't push it. Stay away from Sophie. She's been mine for ten years, and she just moved back and we just reconnected."

"I thought you didn't do relationships."

"I don't. I do Sophie." I stopped stretching and glared at him. "Maybe today isn't a good day for me to be here. I'll go get her, and we'll leave."

"Carter, I'm just giving you a hard time. I saw you two

walking in together, and you never took your eyes off her. Did you really think my mom showing up in the library when you two were in there was a coincidence?"

Yeah, I guessed I should have seen that one coming. Still, I turned to face him and mouthed, "Fuck you."

He let out a throaty chuckle.

Once the kids were well stretched, we divided them into two teams and ran them for almost two hours. When the littlest of our boys kicked the ball and scored, we called the game.

"Score. Awesome kick. That goalie didn't stand a chance," I said as I swung Jeremy up into my arms and held him high above my head so he could fly like Superman. That was when I spotted Sophie standing at the edge of the field watching me. Putting Jeremy down, I looked over at Logan. "I'm heading out. Be back this week."

"Roger that."

Jogging up to Sophie, I smiled, and from the smile on her face, I could tell that she had enjoyed her time as well. Before I could ask her about it, though, she pulled her phone out and brought it to her ear.

"Hey," she said, her eyes dancing to mine and then away again. "Sure. What time?" She paused for a moment. "No, an hour should be fine. I'm out right now, but by the time I get home and get my car, I should get there right about the same time." She paused again. "We'll talk at lunch, see you then." She hung up.

"I guess from the sound of that call lunch is out," Carter said as we climbed into his Jeep.

"Yeah, that was your sister. She invited me to lunch with the girls."

"Maybe dinner then?" His smile was nothing short of charming.

"Yeah, dinner sounds nice."

I could see what my answer had done to him. It was in the smirk on his lips as he started his Jeep and the way he shifted just a bit closer to me as he drove. "Soph, I need to ask you something, and I need you to be honest. If you can't answer right away, I understand." Carter glanced at me. "Are you feeling this thing between us, or is it just me?"

God, that was a loaded question. Yes, I felt it, but that didn't mean I could act on it. He didn't know the real me and didn't want to know the real me. I let out a sigh, and Carter's head turned. I hadn't meant for him to hear that.

His smile vanished. "Never mind, I shouldn't have asked." He narrowed his eyes and put every ounce of his focus into driving.

"Will you stop that?" I asked.

"Stop what?"

"Jumping to conclusions. Assuming you know what I'm feeling or thinking. Take your pick."

"I didn't mean to assume. I just didn't want to push you."

"Listen, Carter, you said for me to think about this, which was what I was doing. It's just like the other night at Sixes when you asked me where I went and then said that you didn't want my excuses. You didn't even give me a chance to try to explain. I hate that." Shoving my hands into my hair, I turned and stared out the window, watching the buildings pass by.

"I didn't mean to make you so angry."

I huffed, choosing silence over saying the wrong thing. I didn't know why I was suddenly so angry. Maybe because he dismissed his question before I had a chance to answer? Maybe because I didn't like the answer I was about to give him? Maybe because I was sick of this hot and cold I was getting from him? Maybe because I knew that telling him I didn't feel it was a lie, or, was I pissed at myself for being a chicken? All of that? None of that? God, I had no clue. When Carter turned into my driveway, I pulled out my keys and then turned to him. "Don't bother getting out, I'm just going to get in my car and go."

"Soph—"

"No, Carter, stop. I told you last night that I'm sorry that I hurt you. I'm not going to give you any excuses as to why I left, after all, you said they're only for my benefit, anyway. But I will say this—a broken heart isn't the worst pain you'll ever face, regret is."

With that, I jumped out, slammed his door, and strode to the side door of my garage. My hands shook so much that once I was in my car, I had to rest my head against the steering wheel. I waited for a few seconds while I tried to catch my breath and ease my aching heart before opening the garage door, pulling out and then heading for Sixes.

It wasn't until I turned onto Kirkman Road that I saw Carter in my rearview mirror. He was a few car lengths behind me, watching me, so I tried to be discreet as I wiped the tears from my cheeks. When I pulled into the bar's parking lot, he slowed and then continued on.

Really, Deputy Lang, not only did you decide what I can and can't say but now you have to follow me to see where I'm going? I'm a fucking adult, I'd appreciate it if people started treating me like one. I had to get my anger under control before I got out of my MINI or I was likely to take it out on the girls.

Waiting a few minutes, I rolled my neck back and forth, took a few deep breaths, and then got out of my car before heading into Sixes.

"She's here!" Stella shouted and stood to give me a hug. "Girl, you and I need to talk," she said sotto voce. "I'm dying to know all about last night. One second, you and my brother were dancing, and the next second"—she made an explosion gesture—"poof."

I didn't say anything, which was probably what caused Stella to stop and stare.

"Wait a minute, have you been crying? There's no crying in fight club."

I placed my hand on her forehead to see if she was okay. "Fight club?"

"Bitch, please, what happens at fight club stays at fight club. Let's go have a seat and chat."

I chose the chair farthest from Stella and shook my head, smiling. She must already be drinking if she was getting her catch phrases wrong.

"Nice try, that woman has tentacles that reach anywhere," Ariel whispered.

"Now, lay it on me. What's the story behind you and my brother, and don't lie. I'd rather you keep us out than lie."

Ughhhh. "What do you know, anything?" I looked mainly at Stella.

"Here's what we know." She tossed a conspiratorial grin around the table. Apparently, this had already been discussed. "Last year, he got drunk—I'm talking totally sloshed—and went on some diatribe about how you can't trust women and how they'll leave you without a word. He kept doing this fucking hand gesture so much that now we do it."

"Poof," They all said while holding up their hand and mimicking an explosion.

"What makes you think that he was referring to me? It could have been anyone."

"Great question. A few months after the whole drunk rambling incident, we were all sitting right here at this exact table and your name came up. You would have thought Carter had seen a ghost. He strode out of here, knocking over drinks and chairs on his way."

Ariel took over, and I turned to her, listening. "Now, you're back, and he spends more than anyone else at an auction just to have dinner and a dance with you."

"Yup," Stella said, making me volley my attention back to her. "And then you both disappear around the same time. Hmmm . . . I wonder what you two were doing." She drummed her nails against the side of her face, waiting for my answer. I could go one of two ways with this. I could tell them that they were forgetting the fact that I'd spent the last ten years in California. Since there was no way that they knew about Carter and I having a relationship when I was a teenager, their assumptions were a huge jump. Or, I could just tell them the truth.

"Fine. I'll tell you. But this stays between us, okay?" Everyone nodded, scooting closer so they didn't miss a word.

It made me want to laugh, I had missed this for the last ten years. But instead, I launched into my explanation. "I met your brother my senior year of high school right after he graduated the academy."

"Uh-huh..." Stella rolled her hands in the air signaling that I needed to get a move on with the story.

"Anyway, one night, I was speeding and he pulled me over. I am not a crying kind of girl, so when he asked me if I knew why he pulled me over, I asked him if he wanted the truth or what I imagined myself saying."

"Ohh, that did it. Carter loves sass," Stella whispered.

"He chose what I imagined, so I told him that I was just trying to keep up with traffic. When he pointed out that it was midnight and the road was deserted, he played right into the punch line. I told him that was why I was speeding, and I had to catch up with everyone else. It was stupid, I know, but we got into this habit of him pulling me over and me giving him some smartass answer as to why I was speeding. Eventually, whenever I saw him, I would just pull over so we could talk. It progressed from there."

"Okay, what the fuck happened then?"

"The day after I turned eighteen I had to leave."

Leo opened her mouth, and I gave her a subtle shake.

Please don't say anything, please. Leo didn't know the truth but she knew there had to be more to the story, I had been too excited about starting at UCF and her moving in with me.

"Yeah, I'm not buying it. There has to be more," Stella said coolly.

"That's the gist of it." It was all I was willing to offer since she told me not to lie.

"Well, okay then. Stella, you got your answer, so why don't we talk about the ladies' motorcycle class that we have coming up on Thursday?" Ariel asked in an attempt to change the subject, but the hairs on the back of my neck still stood on end as Stella refused to tear her gaze away from me.

"Leo and Piper will be teaching the majority of the class, so we'll be there more or less as assistants. When it comes to the driving portion, we'll be paired with one of the students, how does that sound?" Ariel looked at everyone, but I kept my eyes on the table because I could still feel Stella's gaze. "Have you decided whether or not to join us? We have five registered, so with you, we'll each have a partner."

"Yes." I stopped for a second. There was something fulfilling about knowing that just by saying yes, I could make so many people happy. I liked that they wanted to have me around and that they actually cheered all because I said 'yes'. I waited for their deafening roar of excitement to die down before continuing. "I'm gonna give it a try, but I don't see myself on a motorcycle. I'm so girly."

"And we're what? Boys?" I turned to look at Leo when she said that.

"No, that isn't what I meant. Well, that isn't how I meant it. What I mean is that I'm more of a Vespa girl than a Harley girl."

"Fuck no. Vespas might be cute but they have no weight on the highway or with Florida winds. If you are going to ride on two wheels, it needs to be solid." Looking at Leo, I shook my head. She was so different from the girl I remembered. When I left she was controlled by her Pentecostal mother, who was against women cutting their hair, wearing pants, or putting on makeup.

"What would I need if I decided to join your class?"

"Helmet, gloves, boots, and a jacket. I have a few helmets that you could try on, and for the class, you can wear any type of closed-toe shoes and a long-sleeve shirt. You aren't going on the open road."

"But I want real biker stuff, is there somewhere I can get those things?"

"Of course." Leo looked down at her clothes. "I get off at three this week, just come up to Harley and I can help you get whatever you need."

"I'm happy that you're giving it a chance, even if you decide not to ride a motorcycle, you're spending the day with us," Ariel said.

I walked out of Sixes, shaking my head not believing what I had just agreed to do. I, Sophia Kostas, was going to learn how to ride a Harley, what had this world come to?

I had just gotten home and closed my garage door when my doorbell rang. Rolling my eyes, I went to answer it, already having a sinking suspicion that I knew who it was.

"Have you ever been on a motorcycle?"

"No."

His question hit me, and it dawned on me, oh my God, I had just agreed to take a class and I had never even been on a motorcycle.

"Let's go for a ride. Why don't you go change and put on some tennis shoes or boots, I brought a jacket and helmet." He smiled, and his fucking dimple, just one in that left cheek that I hadn't seen in ten years, popped out, and I thought that I must have gone crazy because I was wondering if rice would fit in it.

"You okay, Soph?"

"Huh? Yeah. Oh, sorry. Let me go change." Getting caught fantasizing over weird shit that I'd like to do to him wasn't the best way to start my evening. I quickly changed and then freshened up my makeup because. . . hello . . . I was going to be with Carter, the man was panty-soaking gorgeous. Heading back downstairs, I slid my license, debit card, and phone into my pocket and grabbed my house key.

"I'm ready."

Turning to me, his eyes did a slow sweep of my body before he grabbed my hands and pulled them behind my back. Holding them together with one hand, he moved his body against mine, and swept my hair out of my eyes with his other hand. "Don't close your eyes." His voice was low, his mouth so close to mine that I could almost taste him. If Carter's touch set my skin on fire, his kiss set my soul ablaze.

I wanted this man. I wanted him to take me. It was crazy, but God, I needed him. I had never been so turned on in my entire life. When he pulled away, I wanted to shout and beg him to forgive me for running out of the hotel room and to please give me another chance.

"Let's go." He stepped back, giving me space but not letting go of my hand as he led me out of my house and over to his bike, which was a beautiful royal blue. He unhooked two helmets from the backrest before placing one on top of my head. Sweeping a loose strand of hair out of my face, his callused fingers sent shivers through me. My emotions were raging, and somehow, they all seemed to be forming a knot right between my legs. My thighs clenched as the wave rippled over me.

Carter straddled the bike before holding his hand out to help me on. Placing a foot on the peg, I let him balance me as I swung my leg over so that I was sitting behind him. Scooting in close, I wrapped my arms around his waist and leaned in, resting my head against his back. The pounding from his heartbeat and the way his chest expanded with each breath did something to me, and it all hit me at once.

My Carter was here. Carter, who I never thought that I'd ever see again let alone have him in my arms.

When he started the engine, the vibration from the motor was intoxicating. There was a heady feeling to having this power beneath me and to be straddling Carter at the same time. All I could think about was how it would feel if he made love to me on this bike.

I discovered rather fast that I enjoyed the freedom of being on a bike as it sped down the road and the wind whipped against my face. It was dangerous, and yet, Carter gave me a sense of invincibility just by being near him. With each curve and shift of gears, my excitement grew and my anticipation for the ladies' class got higher.

Over time, I lost my self-awareness of where my hands rested. That was, of course, until his cock grew harder and thicker beneath my hands. With each bump, my forearm shifted across his lap, and the rumbling of the engine kept me constantly touching him. When he pulled into a parking lot after our scenic drive, I couldn't face him, I was embarrassed and aroused.

"I'm sorry." That sounded so lame, but I didn't know what else to say. I mean my hands were just rubbing his cock. From the corner of my eye, I saw him remove his gloves and then bring his hand toward me.

"Look at me, princess." He put a finger under my chin and forced me to look up. "Since reconnecting with you the other night, you've said sorry an awful lot. What are you sorry about now?" I darted my eyes toward his crotch, and he let out a low laugh. "Don't be sorry about that. I hated stopping, but I had promised you dinner." He leaned in and kissed me. That was the precise moment that I understood why people did drugs. They wanted the rush. It was euphoric, and Carter was my crack.

We walked into Rocco's Tacos and grabbed a table outside that overlooked a lake. When the waitress came by, we both ordered chicken tacos.

"Since this is our official first date, what is standard first date talk?" Carter asked me.

"Our first date?"

"Yeah, first date. I told you that I wanted to spend time with you and get to know this Sophie. Then I asked you out, and you said yes. That makes this a date." He winked.

"Okay then, we're probably supposed to talk about boring stuff like the weather or the fact that I'm an only child or that my mom works for Disney or that I'm a writer. Maybe I should tell you that I was born in Orlando. How about you?"

He let out a laugh. "I have one sister, she's a year younger, my parents are divorced but are still friends, neither lives close. I was also born in Florida, Winter Park to be exact. I'm a deputy. Your turn."

"Let's see, my favorite color is yellow, my family is very close—sometimes too close. I'm Greek. I'm fluent in Greek. My favorite movie is *Aladdin,* and when I was in high school I got to be Jasmine at Disney. I guess it's my olive skin and dark hair. Okay, your turn." I let out a laugh at our quid pro quo.

"Like most teenagers in central Florida, I worked at the parks, but I didn't work for Disney, I worked for Universal." I gave him a groan. I was loyal to the mouse. "My favorite color was blue, but now it's the color of your eyes."

"That's cheesy. Are we going to start with the pick-up lines next?"

"I'm serious, I missed your eyes. My favorite movie is any of the Jason Bourne ones. I'm pretty good with Spanish. My sister and I are close. Now you."

My turn was interrupted by the server bringing our dinners.

When I started the conversation back up, I decided on a new topic. "I can't get over all the changes and that there is no more Wet 'n Wild. Where are the locals supposed to go now? Leo and I spent our summers there." I let out a little snicker. "One time, Ian brought a bottle of red food coloring with him, and he poured it into the kiddie pool section. Since it was just food coloring, the filtration system had no clue anything was wrong with the water. Oh my God, it was mayhem! Everyone was searching for who was bleeding. Leo, Kayson, and I were sitting back laughing."

"I'm surprised that we never met sooner, I spent many summers at Wet 'n Wild, but I usually hung out at the base of the Der Stuka." Carter wiggled his eyebrows as if I should understand.

"I don't get it. I never rode the Der Stuka, holy hell that slide was almost vertical, Kayson and Ian said that their butts lifted off the slide every time they went down. There was no way I was riding that, plus half the girls got off with their asses showing because they had massive wedgies or they'd lost their bikini tops." Carter's smile got bigger, telling me that was precisely why he'd hung out at the bottom of the slide. "You pervert. You were just trying to get your rocks off to some poor flat-chested girl."

"Hey, don't judge. I was like twelve, how else was I supposed to see those things? And don't tell me you didn't get up to your own trouble. You were probably looking for some Italian in a Speedo."

I thought for a moment. "Okay, there was this one time I had a major crush on one of the lifeguards. Every time I was at the park, I'd choose a chair in his area, swim in his area, and well, just be an overall flirt. His name was Julio." I batted my eyelashes as I said his name for emphasis. "Anyway, it didn't take long for Julio to realize that I was trying to get his attention, so on his breaks, we would hang out and talk. Well, until Kayson noticed and told his brothers."

Carter was smirking, probably imagining exactly how that panned out when he said, "I'm afraid to ask, but at the same time, I want to know." Carter's smile widened.

"The dipshits had T-shirts made that read, '*Nunca encuentran tu cuerpo.*'"

Carter let out a laugh. "Oh my God, that is classic. I'm assuming that Julio spoke Spanish."

"Yep, he was from Puerto Rico and was fluent. There's nothing like having four large boys wearing the statement 'They'll never find your body' to help with a girl's dating life. Needless to say, that was the end of Julio and me."

By the time we finished our dinner and I was strapping the helmet back on, it was after eight. I waited for Carter to get on the bike before climbing on behind him and then slid my hands around his waist, pulling myself tight against his body. I held on, hating that our night was coming to an end.

The ride home was shorter than the ride there, and in no time Carter pulled up in front of my house and helped me off the bike. I wrestled with ideas in my head, I didn't want him to leave and I didn't want to lead him on. When finally, I decided screw it. "Want to come in?" I asked as I inserted my key into the door, which kept me from facing him. I tried to convince myself that I was only being nice. Twisting the knob, I couldn't hold back my smile when I realized that he was following me inside. My mind moved a million miles a minute as I tried to think of ways to get him to keep following me. If I went upstairs, would he follow me?

I dropped my keys on the side table and slowly turned around. His hungry lips were immediately on mine, and he pressed me against the wall before I was able to take a single step up the stairs toward my bedroom. His knee slipped between my legs. I found myself hot and wet as I pulled him even closer to me. He held his hands firmly around my hips until I was riding his thigh. The hot flush crawled up my neck, my entire face burned as if I had been out in the sun all day. Every muscle in my body went tense as Carter guided my movements, firmly rocking me against his leg so that my clit rubbed against my jeans with each tug and push. He tugged the bottom of my earlobe between his teeth and lightly bit, sending warm sparks racing through my body. With every ounce of strength that I could muster, I held onto him. He pulled back to stare into my eyes just as a rush of release broke free inside me.

"I think I need to see that again," Carter moaned against my neck just before he swept me up into his arms.

Chapter Eight

CARTER

A trickle of sweat slid down my back. I didn't think I was this nervous the night that I lost my virginity when I was fifteen.

"Princess, where's your room?" I pressed my lips to hers, sweeping my tongue into her mouth as I carried her up the stairs, using the wall to steady me.

"To the left," she panted.

I entered her room, and all pretenses of having this under control were lost. I was in Sophie's room. Sophie Kostas.

"Give me a second, okay?" Sophie tapped my arms for me to put her down. When I did, she walked over to her dresser, pulled something from the top drawer, and then shut herself in her bathroom.

Slipping off my shoes, I rubbed the back of my neck, then brought my hand down and fumbled with the watch's wristband. Fuck, I was jittery. I turned around, taking in her room. The pale yellow of the room wasn't girly, but it was soft. The scent was a mix of flowers, I wasn't sure which ones, but I knew that I'd never forget the fragrance.

I looked up when she opened the door again, wearing a T-shirt and if she was wearing something else I didn't notice because she was absolutely perfect. She licked her lips, and in three strides I was next to her, pulling her toward the bed until she was lying in the center. Her olive skin was a stark contrast to the pale yellow of the comforter. As I rubbed my face against hers, it turned a soft red from the stubble of my unshaven chin. Something about the marks I left on her was thrilling, a claiming, and I found myself getting harder than I had ever been before.

After crawling up beside her, I rested on one elbow. Placing small kisses along her arms, I brought her hands to my lips before kissing each finger and then sucking them one by one into my mouth.

"Carter, please. I want you." She pulled her lip between her teeth.

"Oh God, Sophie. Stop biting that lip, I'm the only one that should do that." With my thumb, I pulled her bottom lip out and moved in for a deeper kiss.

"Carter."

She said my name as a sigh when I slid my hand to the hem of her shirt and skimmed the lace edge of her panties. I moved the elastic to the side and slid one finger to her core, lightly tracing her folds. She bucked at my touch, and I pulled back to give her a second.

Sliding my hand back down to her panties, I slowly started working them off. Pushing up, I sat on my haunches and looked down at her, she was beautiful. Moving to the bottom of the bed, I dragged her panties with me until they were off her and she was open and inviting. I wanted to see her, all of her, but when I reached for the hem of her shirt to lift it off, she held it down.

"I want to leave it on."

"Please, I need to see you, touch you," I was begging, I was desperate for her.

"I don't like having my breasts touched." She didn't meet my eyes when she said that, which gave me pause. More than anything I wanted to take in every inch of her bared body but something told me to slow down, that if I asked again, she would bolt.

So, I moved back down her body, urging her legs apart and dropping my mouth close to her sex. "Does my princess like to have her pussy eaten?"

She let out a whimper at my words as I spread her lips apart. "So. Fucking. Hot." With one long stroke of my tongue, her nails were biting into my scalp and she was pressing my head down into her warm center. "That's right, baby, I'm home." Each lick and twirl of my tongue had her gasping. I'd never been big on eating a girl out. I used my cock and my fingers to get the job done, and hell, both bordered on magical. But watching Sophie's climax build and listening to her tiny moans as she stretched to find her release had me fucking reevaluating my stance. She was close and just watching her had me ready to explode. Sliding one finger inside her, I stilled at the feel of how fucking tight she was and then added a second. Holy shit, I wasn't going to last. I moved my fingers, stretching her, and then licked every drop that poured from her. When her body tightened with the first pulse of her orgasm, I was moaning with her. I'd never imagined finding satisfaction at just watching someone else, but God damn, she was a fucking work of art when she came. Waiting for her grip on my fingers to relax, I rolled off the bed, watching her as I pulled a condom from my wallet, tossed it onto the bed, and pulled my clothes off.

Stretching out next to her, I swept my fingers up her arms and watched the hairs prickle. With a pull, I rolled her on top of me and set her on my legs, she was bare, exposed, and straddling me, it was the hottest fucking thing ever. She leaned forward, pressing hot, open-mouthed kisses along my jaw. She pulled back then unwrapped the condom and slid it down my throbbing cock.

I held myself at the base while she lifted her hips and slowly sank down on me.

Her eyes fluttered shut, and she let loose a half-moan, half-sigh, as I urged her to lift just the smallest amount before sliding down again. Each stroke had me writhing as much as she was, her head swung in abandonment as she gave herself over to the ecstasy. Sophie twisted her hips, and I was a teenager again on prom night. Since hearing her name again after all this time, I'd been in no mood to go out with any women. The months of no action except for *PALMela HANDerson* had me on the edge of blowing deep inside her. "Holy fucking shit, slow down, babe." She looked at me with an evil grin and only quickened her strokes, up and down. Her nails trailed down my chest before she leaned back and moved her hands to rest behind her on my thighs so that she was open. I could see my dick diving deep into her body and disappearing, and that was all it took for me to come. Each thrust of her hips matched my throb of release until I had nothing left. She fell forward and rested her head against my chest, my cock still inside her as I swept her sweat-soaked hair away from her face. I listened to the sounds of her breaths, and it had my dick getting hard again. Usually, I was like most guys and needed a break between orgasms to build up a little reservoir, but my cock had become a freethinker when Sophie was around and was doing his own thing.

She let out a giggle.

"Should I be offended that you're laughing while I'm still inside you?" I placed a kiss on the tip of her nose.

She laughed again. "No, it kind of tickles."

"What does?" I raised an eyebrow.

"You. I can feel you getting bigger and harder."

"You can, can you? Want to know what else you're going to feel?"

~

ALMOST TWO HOURS LATER, I was leaning back against Sophie's headboard and she was in my arms. "Okay, Miss Story Teller, why don't you tell me a story?"

She leaned back, and I could practically see the wheels in her head working as she tried to concoct a story.

"Well, once upon a time"—she gave me a wicked smile —"there was this man who worked in a meat packing plant in Philadelphia, and every day, he would hang the meat, and as a workout, he would punch it. *POW. POW.*" Her hands waved as she told the story, which had me pondering if she could still talk if I taped her hands down. "Well, one day, this guy sees him and says, 'You'd be a great boxer,' so he starts training." I let out my first laugh, trying to figure out where the fuck this story was going. "He gets good, really good, and starts winning all of these boxing matches. Eventually, he goes on to become the heavyweight champion of the world. And as he is standing in the center of the ring, holding this giant god-awful-no-sense-of-style-what-so-ever belt above his head, he looks out into the crowd for his wife, but he can't find her. So, he starts shouting, 'Adrian! Yo, Adrian!'"

I grabbed her and pulled her to the bed tickling her. The sound of her laughter warmed every part of my soul.

"I think that story has already been written." The look of feigned shock on her face was adorable. "But we can always name our firstborn Rocky." I lowered my lips to hers, and my dick was ready to go again.

Chapter Nine

SOPHIE

*a*fter zipping my new black leather ankle boots with silver spikes that resembled skulls, I pulled down the hem of my jeans and then walked over to my mirror. I couldn't hold back the smile, I looked a little badass sporting the biker look. The leather vest that Leo encouraged me to buy only added to the overall effect. I also bought a jacket, rain gear, gloves, and helmet for today's class, fully expecting to fall even deeper in love with riding.

The smell of coffee hit me as I turned to see Carter coming into my room holding two mugs. Last night . . . it was so fucking awesome. I can't even explain this feeling I have for him. I am so screwed.

"You look hot. Holy shit, can you wear just those boots and vest tonight and nothing else, it really shows off your tits."

I pulled back at his words.

"What, baby? I'm sorry, I was just playing with you."

"I know. It's just early. I need to get going, it's going to be a long day." I stood on tiptoes and placed a kiss on Carter's lips. "There's a spare key in the drawer in the kitchen island. Will you be here tonight?"

"Do you want me here?"

"Yes. I'd like us to talk." I needed to explain everything to him. "But more than just talking, I need you to let me explain things."

"Okay." He nodded slowly, not taking his eyes from mine. "I'll be here."

Leaning into him, I soaked in his body heat and strength, I was going to need it tonight. Throwing everything into the back of my MINI Cooper Countryman, I pressed the remote to close my garage door then pulled out of my driveway. I looked into my rearview mirror, trying to picture a Harley parked in the driveway. How would two Harleys look there? Shit. Two? Fuck. Two, one mine and one Carter's. I was delusional. Carter was the kind of man who wanted a family. He deserved more than I would ever be able to give him.

Parking in front of Historic Harley Davidson where Leo and the girls were hosting their first ever all-ladies motorcycle safety class, I had my first flicker of apprehension. I, Sophia Christine Kostas, was going to be a biker chick? I jumped at the sound of a knock on my window and turned to see Stella reaching for my door handle. I pressed unlock then leaned over to grab my helmet, leaving the jacket and rain gear in my car.

"You came, you came. I'm so happy." Stella pulled me out of my car and wrapped her hands around my arm. "Girl, I let it slide yesterday because I could see something was wrong but seriously, what is up with you and Carter? He texted me just moments before you walked into Sixes yesterday and asked me to let him know when you left because he wanted to take you to dinner. He and I text each other practically every day, but suddenly, he is putting a smiley emoji at the end of his texts. What the fuck? What man puts a smiley emoji at the end of their text?"

It didn't seem as if she really wanted me to answer so I just stayed quiet and allowed her to keep rambling.

"Got to be honest with you, there is something about you that makes my brother want to be a better man. And let me tell you, anyone that can wrap my brother around their little pinkie the way you obviously have must have some mad skills, I need lessons. I swear that man has totally changed since you returned, I haven't seen him act like this in well . . . well . . . ten years. You must teach me the ways old wise one, I am ready to learn." Stella let out a laugh that sounded more like a cackle. "Whatever secret it is that you have, once you share it, the men in Central Florida are fucked."

"Seriously, I have no clue what in the hell you are talking about. Your brother and I are just friends." I wasn't sure who I was trying to convince—Stella or myself, especially since last night proved that Carter and I were more than friends.

"Righhttt."

The heat in my cheeks rose. "Can we keep this just between us for now?"

"Abso-fuckin-lutely . . . not. Told you once, tell you again. We girls got no secrets. But it doesn't leave us and we will fight to the death. I will, however, tell you that it isn't something we need to talk about now." Stella and I walked into a small classroom where several women were already gathered. It was nice seeing some familiar faces. Leo, Ariel, Stella, and their friends all wore black leather vests exactly like the one Leo convinced me to buy. But their vests all had embroidery on the back, wings with the front of a motorcycle, and orchids.

The flower was a bit confusing at first, but then I remembered they called themselves the Iron Orchids. I still couldn't picture these women as part of a motorcycle club. I'd read a few romance books about MC clubs, and although they were sexy as hell and great for a night with the vibrator, it wasn't exactly the life I'd truly want to lead.

I looked around at the other students and smiled when I saw Juliet, the tiny radio host from the auction the other night, and chose the seat next to her. "She roped you in, too?"

"Yep."

Our group was eclectic. There was a kindergarten teacher, a dog groomer, a college student, and a tattoo artist.

After the introductions, Piper started the class with laws of the road and motorcycle misconceptions but paused when her phone rang. She almost ignored it, but when she looked at the caller ID, she answered. I was like everyone else, nosy.

"Yes. Thank you for letting me know, sir. Yes, sir. Thank you." When she disconnected and stood, she didn't say anything at all. She just stood there opening and closing her mouth until Ariel's curiosity had gotten the better of her.

"Well, don't just stand there like some largemouth bass. What the hell was that all about?"

"That was Captain Getty. He was calling to congratulate me on my new position as a motorcycle deputy. I report Monday morning." She threw her hands in the air and jumped around.

We all cheered. I saw a tear roll down Piper's cheek as we all abandoned our spots and went to congratulate her. That only lasted a minute before she was right back in instructor mode, ordering us back to our seats and then resuming her discussion on how to handle the bike during heavy traffic and how some states allowed motorcyclists to use the center paint strip but not Florida.

At ten, Leo led us outside where each of us was positioned next to a bike. Since no one was standing next to me, I assumed that she was going to be my partner.

"You have in front of you a Street 500, it is a 500cc engine, the cc stands for cylinder capacity, which is the size of the cylinders." That earned her a blank look from everyone in the class, and she smiled, explaining, "The bigger the cylinder, the more fuel it can burn, which also gives you more power. The 500 is Harley's smallest engine. The bike in front of you weighs approximately five hundred pounds dry, that means bare, without oil, fuel, nada. Before straddling your bike, we're going to do a walk around and examine the tires and lights."

I was in a daze as I tried to take in all the information as Leo explained that no matter how many times we rode, we should always check our bikes before riding off. A motorcycle was like a mini earthquake always in motion and things would constantly wiggle loose. When she was done, it was time to get on the bike, which I was more nervous about than I thought I would be. It was totally different when the realization hit that you were going to be riding around on two wheels.

"Straddle your bikes and place your hands on the handle bars, do not turn the engines on," Leo said as she came to stand next to me.

For the next thirty minutes, we learned about shifting gears, braking, and using the throttle before moving on to walking the bike around the coned-off course area. The motherfucker was heavy, I could already sense that by five o'clock tonight, when the class was over, my arms were going to be killing me.

"Okay, kickstands down." Leo instructed.

"Harley has bar-b-que and drinks for all y'all or there's McDonalds at the corner, and of course, the mall is just down the road. Whatever you decide, let's meet back in one hour." Ariel clapped her hands a few times, breaking the class for lunch.

"Come on, let's eat." I pulled Ariel with me and headed toward the giant garage doors where a tent was set up with smokers and coolers. I stopped when a pair of ice blue eyes and a sexy smirk caught my attention.

After fixing my plate, I headed over to a table where Carter was sitting and joined him. "What are you doing here?"

"I wanted to come up and see how you were enjoying the class. Like it?"

I shook my shoulders to ease the pain that was already building just from holding the bike up. "Yeah. But the bikes are a lot heavier than I had imagined. I'm not sure I have the upper body strength."

Carter's strong grip squeezed the muscles along my neck-line. "Believe it or not, it will build up fast. You're on Harley's lightest bikes, you don't want anything lighter or you won't be able to control the bike when a gust of wind or even a semi-truck blows by you."

Lightest? I couldn't handle heavier. I would just finish the class and then tell the girls that I'd think about it. I wouldn't have to commit immediately.

Our table shook as Stella and Leo sat with us. Everly, Vivian, Piper, and Ariel sat at the table to our left. Within a few minutes, the other five women from our class had joined us.

When we were finished eating, I stood to throw my garbage away and Carter's strong hand snaked around my waist.

"What are you doing?" I pushed his hand away before the others noticed.

"You look so fucking hot in this vest."

"Shhh, go home and take a cold shower."

"Wait, I brought something." Carter leaned under the table and pulled out a paper bag.

Stella practically climbed over the others to grab it from him. "Oh my God, I love you. You're the best brother in the entire world. I know what these are, and if there is chocolate in there, they couldn't have come at a better time, if you get my meaning."

"Seriously, Stella? They aren't for you, they're for Piper." He turned to her, smiling. "Kayson called me and told me. Congratulations."

Piper stood and hugged him as we all applauded her again.

"What's in the bag?" I leaned over, trying to catch a peek.

Stella was already unpacking the boxes. "Only the best cupcakes in the fucking world, the lady who bakes these has won the cupcake challenge on The Food Network like a bazillion times."

Leaning my head back against Carter, I looked up at him and surrendered, the man was so thoughtful. I'd been hiding my feelings from the girls, from Carter, and even from myself. Smiling up at him, I said, "That was sweet."

When he leaned down and gave me a peck, I met him and kissed him back.

Of course, Stella let out a wolf whistle followed by, "Get a room."

"Well, actually we have. . ."

I elbowed Carter in the chest before he could say anything more, but Stella had already moved on.

"Let me tell you something, having these cupcakes has saved me from going postal. I went to grab a snack out of the vending machines, and fuck it all to hell if there wasn't one single piece of chocolate in the damn thing, but there were all these damn Cracker Jack boxes gleaming front and center. I thought it was some twisted joke." She paused, looked thoughtful, and then started right back in. "Why in the hell are they putting prizes in Cracker Jacks? Isn't getting caramel popcorn prize enough? Someone needs to get on the ball and put prizes in my Tampax box. Congratulations! You won a free Snickers, now stop being a bitch."

Carter shook his head, clearly used to his sister's rampages. We were still laughing at Stella as he gave me a hug goodbye, and the group headed back to the riding area.

Chapter Ten

CARTER

*P*arking in front of the community center, I opened my phone's web browser and did a quick search. Finding the name of the lawyer I needed, I called and made an appointment to meet with him. I was in love with Sophie, so I needed to do this. Once I hung up, I set my watch's alarm to go off in four hours. This morning when I had left Sophie's house, I ran to Publix to grab steaks for dinner and then took them back to her house so I could let them marinate. Before meeting her for lunch, I swung by my condo and picked up my grill. At the rate I was going, there wouldn't be much stuff left in my condo by the end of the month.

Getting out of my Jeep, I saw several of the kids on the swings, but it was three boys that were trying to hide behind a giant oak tree that drew my attention. They thought they were being inconspicuous, but in all actuality, they were triggering my deputy instincts. So, I did what any good deputy would do—I snuck up on them.

All three of them were too focused on a phone to notice me. Shit. They were probably watching porn on the internet, damn it. They were way too young for that shit, about nine years old. Quietly gliding up behind them, I said, "What you doing, boys?" TJ, the one with the phone, shoved it behind his back. Really, dude? Like that wasn't obvious.

"Nothing, Carter. Just talking." Shit, I can't remember that kid's name.

Holding out my hand to them. "Hand me the phone. What were you looking at?"

"Nothing," TJ said. The other two shook their heads.

"Nothing? The three of you boys were looking at a blank screen on a phone? Whose phone is this anyway?"

"My brother's." TJ raised his hand.

"Does he know you have it?"

"No. Please don't tell him."

"Then I suggest you tell me what you were doing." I rested my hands on my hips in total full-on deputy mode.

"Please, Coach Carter, we were just trying to help TJ get even with his brother. He keeps pulling mean tricks on him, and TJ's dad just laughs it off and tells TJ to toughen up, so we were just helping him come up with ideas."

"What kind of pranks has your brother been pulling?"

"He super glued all my underwear closed. You know, that opening I use when I go pee?"

"Yeah, I know the opening." I fought to hold back my laugh.

"And he filled my bed with those white things that come in boxes, those things to keep stuff from breaking when the mailman drops it."

"Styrofoam peanuts?" Or as I liked to call it, ghost shit.

"Yeah, those. There were thousands. I had them sticking everywhere. I couldn't get them off me."

"So, what are you boys trying to do with the phone?"

"I asked my sister what she would do," Matt, the oldest of

the three said. "She told me to change all the names in his phone contact list. So, that's what we were doing."

"That's genius. Your brother is how old, TJ?"

"He's thirteen. Please don't tell him."

"I won't say a thing. But a word of advice, the three of you sneaking behind this tree made it pretty obvious that you were up to something. If your brother sees you, he might come over to find out what you're up to." I handed him back the phone. "Oh, and if he keeps pulling pranks on you, try gluing the caps to his shampoo, deodorant, and cologne shut. My sister did that to me once, and it drove me crazy."

"Thanks, Carter." TJ held out his fist, and I gave him a bump.

After checking in with Denise, I headed for the center of the playground, where the grass was most lush and green. It was Bee's favorite spot. Spying her at a distance, lost in her daydreams.

"So, what do you see today?" I asked as I squatted down beside her.

"Hey, Carter. I see a castle."

"A big castle?"

"A pretty castle. There are enough bedrooms for me, my mommy, a daddy, and brothers and sisters. There is also a ginormous pool and a dog."

What she called a castle most kids called a home, wow, the things we take for granted. I made a mental note to talk to Denise and learn more about Bee.

"What kind of dog, can you tell?"

"Yep. A small one, it has long floppy ears. It looks like Lady from the movie *Lady and the Tramp*."

"Oh, a Cocker Spaniel."

"I guess so. Her name is Cricket."

"Cricket? Why Cricket?"

"Because I'm Bee, my mom is Katy Bug, so the dog needs a bug name."

"Ahh, that makes perfect sense. You are absolutely adorable." I said as I stood up, ready to head to the basketball courts. It was at that moment; I decided that I didn't want a daughter like Bee. She was going to be a heartbreaker. My words had made her blush, and now she was peeking at me while keeping her lashes resting against her cheek.

Something in Bee's reaction made the whole situation hit me; I had officially lost it. I was thinking about my future kids with a woman, who I had just reconnected with.

I moved to the courts where I picked up a game of basketball with some of the older kids.

"What's up? Who wants to play?"

We divided into two teams, and I appointed TJ's older brother as the other team's captain. The game was close. TJ's words that his dad kept telling him to toughen up' rolled around in my head.

"Okay, we need to distract the other team, does the captain have a girlfriend?" I asked my teammates.

"No," one of his friends on my team answered. "He likes Stacy but she won't give him the time of day."

"Stacy who comes here?" I asked for clarification.

"Yep. She only comes here when she's visiting her dad and won't give him her number."

"Jordan—" I said to one of my teammates, "—you take the ball and pass it to Gavin. When Gavin gets ready to throw it, you say Stacy's name. Don't point, don't say hi, just say her name. It's all we need to win the game. Ready?" We brought our hands in to the center. "On three. One, two, break." Just like clockwork, Jordan dribbled, took one step forward, and passed to Gavin. Just as Gavin was getting ready to shoot, Jordan called, "Stacy," and TJ's brother turned his head, missing the block, the ball swished right into the hoop.

"No fair!" He shouted.

"Why not?" I wrapped my arm around his shoulder.

"He said Stacy."

"You've got to learn to toughen up." The kid glared at me. "By the way, I spent some time with your brother. He and I made a list of pranks. Some of them we'll hold on to for when Stacy comes back. She should be here next week, isn't that when she's at her dad's again?" His face turned redder. "If I were you, I'd be nice to my little brother. Most girls find it hot when guys are nice to young kids. Believe me, I used to get all the girls just by being sweet to my sister, and she was a brat. Girls eat that stuff up." I handed him back the basketball when my alarm went off. "Sorry, guys, gotta go."

"Hot date, Coach?"

"Wouldn't you like to know?"

"Ahhh, come on, tell us something."

"I'll tell you that she's beautiful." I smiled and headed out. Honestly, Sophie was more than just beautiful, she was . . . everything.

Chapter Eleven

SOPHIE

hree hours later, my arms were killing me, and I was finally sitting in the classroom while Piper was reviewing the driving laws. At four o'clock, we were each handed our test papers and were told to begin. It only took me about thirty minutes to complete the whole thing, and when I looked up, I freaked. I was the first one finished, and it scared me. Fuck, I couldn't be the first one. That had to be a bad omen—I had screwed up, I had wrong answers. Going back over each question on the test, I re-read slowly, checking, and double-checking until the scraping sound of chairs sliding across the hard floor gave me the telltale sign that the other women were finished as well.

We all left the room while our tests were graded, which only took about fifteen minutes.

Leo stood at the front of the room ready to speak. "Well, I'm excited to announce that all of you passed." We clapped. "And we're all getting out early." We clapped even louder. "Before we hand out certificates, I want to remind everyone that you'll need to take these to the DMV to have the motorcycle endorsement added to your license. Also, we"—Leo pointed to herself, Ariel, Stella, and the other members of Iron Orchids—"get together as a group to ride, we'd love to have you join us. If you're interested, please speak to Vivian or come up to Sixes Bar and Grill anytime. Vivian owns the place, and that's our go-to hang out."

Leo finished speaking, and Piper stepped to the center. She called out our names and handed us our forms. We waited while each person was called and applauded each other before saying our goodbyes.

I was so fucking sore but after spending the day with the girls, I realized that I really liked them and would have loved to join them. I could see myself riding, and after my day on the back of Carter's bike, I wanted that feeling of freedom. But I knew that if I did that, I would spend every night in pain. Fuck, sometimes I hated my life. It wasn't fair.

"So, what did you think?" Stella asked from behind me, oblivious to my internal pity party.

"I loved it, but I just don't have the upper body strength. My arms are killing me." I rubbed my biceps as she gave me a critical sweep. If she asked me why a seemingly healthy woman in her prime was complaining about a little light workout, I would have to lie to her. I needed to tell Carter before I told anyone else.

"Bitch, you aren't getting off that easy. We'll build a fucking sidecar for you to ride in. We just want you to hang out with us."

"I have a better idea." Leo fell into step beside us and tugged my hand, pulling me from the room.

"Better than chocolate and tampons?" Stella asked. "Because that was a pretty ingenious marketing idea."

"That was pretty good," Ariel said, joining our group.

The clatter of heels echoed as the others followed behind me. Leo stopped in front of an electric-blue motorcycle, which was the same color as Carter's and about the same size as the one the girls rode but this one had two wheels in back and one in front.

"It's a Freewheeler. It does everything that our bikes do, but no need for upper body strength. You still have to get your motorcycle endorsement, though."

I stepped up on the peg and straddled the bike. It felt like a motorcycle, but when I let go, there was no need to use my arms to hold it upright.

"Will they let me test drive it around the lot?"

"Mike, we're taking this Freewheeler outside, just going through the course," Leo yelled as she ran toward an office. She came back holding a key fob. "Let me get it outside for you."

Hairs on the back of my neck rose, and excitement purred through me as the engine roared to life. For once, I wasn't going to have to be the one to make the sacrifice. I wasn't going to have to lose out on what I wanted all because of my lot in life.

When Leo got off and I straddled the bike again, I knew that this was it. I rolled the throttle and went faster than we had in class. I loved the wind in my face. Rolling to a stop, I stalled the thing out and everyone laughed.

"Welcome to the world of being a new motorcycle rider. People will lose their fucking minds when you do this on the road. It's really funny," Stella explained.

When all was said and done, my checking account was a lot lighter, and I could pick up my bike in the morning.

When I got to my house, all I wanted was a long, hot bath, but as soon as I opened my car door, I smelled someone grilling, and my stomach rumbled. Walking onto the back deck, I couldn't hold back the smile at the sight of Carter holding a bottle of beer and flipping steaks.

"Hey, when did I get a grill?" I walked out on to my back deck and greeted him.

"When I ran to my condo and got it. It's the only way that I know how to cook." He leaned down and placed a kiss on my lips. "So, how'd it go?"

"I liked it. I need to go to the DMV tomorrow to get the endorsement added to my license before I can do anything, but I really had fun, and I love the girls."

"I'm glad. We can do the DMV tomorrow. You want to rest while I finish these?"

"I'm going to go change, be right back."

Walking into my bedroom, I shut my door, locked it, and stood in front of my mirror while I examined my left arm. I was afraid to take off my compression sleeve, so I grabbed an oversized sweatshirt and a pair of cutoff sweats. I let out a moan of relief when I unhooked my bra, happy to have that thing off. Pinning my hair back, I scrubbed my face to remove all the dirt and exhaust from today's activities. When I went back downstairs, I curled up into a chair at the table. Dinner was delicious, but honestly, it didn't matter. I was so sore and exhausted that I fell asleep sitting upright.

"Come on, princess, let's go upstairs."

I woke the next morning sweating. Okay, I usually was soaked with sweat, night sweats were terrible, but that morning I was even hotter. It was a combination of the slow movement from Carter's chest and the soft wisp of warm air from every breath that he took that warmed a different part of me. If I didn't do something, I would be stripping this man and riding him like a bronco. As tempting as that was, every muscle in my body hurt, and I doubted I would be riding anything like a bronco anytime soon.

So, instead, I slipped from the bed and headed to the bathroom. After locking the door, I turned on the shower, stripped, and stepped under the lukewarm spray. It was only then that I allowed the sound of the water to drown out the noise of my sobs at the thought of how he would look at me after I told him. I stood in the pouring stream, washing my hair while I cried and worked through how to handle everything. I didn't want to lose him, but it wasn't fair to him. He deserved children, he'd be such an awesome father. He deserved a wife that wasn't broken.

Stepping out of the shower, I wrapped myself in my giant terrycloth robe and towel dried my hair before opening the door.

Carter was gone.

He had left. The indent in the bed where I'd left his gorgeous body laying opened a giant fissure inside me. Numbly, I moved to my closet fighting to restrain myself from going back to bed and wrapping myself up in the covers that an hour ago hugged both of us. I quickly slipped on a jersey dress. When I reemerged, Carter was standing in front of me, holding two cups of coffee.

"I thought you'd left."

"Not on your life." He held out one of the mugs, which I took gratefully. "You aren't getting rid of me that easy." He smiled. "So, what's on the schedule for today?"

"DMV, then practice my mad motorcycle skills."

"Are you getting a motorcycle?" he asked excitedly.

I nodded. "Already bought one. I just have to go pick it up."

"You did? Why didn't you tell me? Did you get a Sportster like Ariel and Stella?"

"You'll have to wait and see. So, what's on your schedule for today?"

"I need to run home and change, and if you don't mind, grab some extra clothes. What if I drop you off at the DMV because it will take you a while, then I can run home and when I'm finished I can circle back and get you? Afterward, we can go get your new bike."

"What, take my car?"

"Or we can take my Jeep."

"Your Jeep is here? I didn't even see it."

"Kayson took me to get it. How tired were you yesterday when you got home? You parked right next to it."

"Very. Okay, sounds like a plan. Let me change into biker clothes."

Closing the door to my dressing area, I stopped when my phone rang and moved back out to grab it. Seeing Leo's name appear, I swiped the screen and answered.

"Talk to me." I tried to make my voice sound deep.

"Hey, SoHo, girls' night out tonight. We're celebrating Piper getting on motors. Sixes. Have Carter drop you off at seven."

"Seven at Sixes?" I replied. It sounded like a damn riddle.

"No. Sixes and seven." I could just picture Leo shaking her head.

"Love ya. Bye." I disconnected and then headed downstairs to where Carter was waiting for me.

Jumping into his Jeep, I couldn't kick the feeling that I was living in a dream. This couldn't be real. It was so normal, and I was anything but normal. I had imagined having a devoted man to do things with, to wake up with and make plans with, but I never saw it as a reality.

When Carter pulled into the DMV, I opened the door, but he didn't let go of my hand.

"Come here, baby."

I turned to face him and he brought his mouth to mine, smiling against my lips. When he pulled back, he was still wearing that smile.

I got out, waving goodbye to him as I walked inside to find wall-to-wall people waiting. I was going to be here for more than half of the day. Resigned, I pulled a number and found a place to sit. An hour later, and only slightly closer to my turn, my phone dinged.

. . .

CARTER: On my way.

ME: No hurry. I'm number W-474 and they just called W-398.

CARTER: Ugh. I hate that place. We'll go to lunch afterward.

ME: Sounds good.

CLOSING OUT THE TEXT MESSAGE, I went back to Pinterest and scrolled through funny memes on my phone. I was not sure if it was a crackle in the air or if the Earth tilted in its axis but whatever it was, I knew he was here before I ever saw him. Maybe it was his eyes that I could feel, the way they looked deep into me as if they saw deep inside of me, or maybe it was my heart just recognizing his. Whatever it was, I looked up to see his mesmerizing blue eyes focused on me and the corners of his mouth pulled up into a tiny smile.

"Hello, Daddy, come and sit on Momma's lap."

I turned to the woman on my left who had said that, but she didn't notice me staring at her because she was too busy seriously eye fucking Carter. My Carter. This possessive, jealous monster that I didn't even know I possessed came out of me. As he got closer, she started preening, she pulled down the front of her shirt. I looked around to see if anyone else was watching this shit, they weren't. I also realized that the only open chair was on the other side of twatwaffle. There was no way in hell I was going to have him sit there. Glancing her way, I shook my head. She was already moving newspapers that someone had left in the seat as invitation for him to sit.

"Excuse me," I said with the sweetest smile on my face. "Do you mind scooting down a seat so that my fiancé can sit next to me?" I tilted my head in a challenge.

Yeah, that's right bitch, I heard you and saw you. And no, I'm not going to let him sit between us.

She gave me a wicked smile, slid down a seat, and smiled. "Sure, he can sit here," she said, patting the seat where she had just been sitting before tilting her attention to Carter. "I kept it warm for you."

Carter cupped my face, and before he could turn to sit, I slid over into the chair and smiled at her. "Thanks. You're a doll."

I couldn't miss Carter's low chuckle as he leaned over to plant a kiss on my cheek. "So, what number are they on now, fiancée?"

At that moment, I just wanted to smack the living shit right out of him. Not because he'd actually done anything wrong. No, it was more out of my own embarrassment. Fuck. Why did the man have to have supersonic hearing?

"Oh, don't scowl, I liked it." Carter's breath tickled my neck as he spoke. "You look all cute when you get jealous."

I turned my body away from him and twisted my head back to stare at him at the same time. Right then I probably resembled Regan from the Exorcist when she turns her head at the priest just before she spits pea green soup all over him. If Carter was wise, he'd let the whole thing drop.

But he wasn't wise.

"Admit it." He leaned over and bumped his shoulder into mine. "You like me. You like me." His voice was in a sing songy, annoying-as-fuck pitch.

"I'm calling a Lyft or Uber."

"Relax, I'm just teasing. You have to give me something every now and then."

My number flashed on the overhead screen, and I stood. "I do give you something, and as I recall, you like it very much." I looked over to make sure that Ho White who'd been sitting next to me drooling over Carter could hear. "In fact, you like it so much that you beg me to give it to you," I said and glanced down at his crotch before heading through the doors to the back area to meet with one of the DMV agents.

Surprisingly, it only took about thirty minutes for everything to get processed, me to get a new license, and for Carter and I to be walking out the door.

Once we were out, I let Carter know about the girls' plans for a night out to celebrate Piper. He didn't argue or get possessive as most guys did in movies, he leaned over and placed a kiss on my lips.

"I'll drop you off and pick you up. That way I know you're safe."

Chapter Twelve

SOPHIE

....

arter's fingers tightened around my hip, securing me next to him as we walked through the door at Sixes. I paused and couldn't believe the turn my life had taken. I needed to stop and search for my fairy godmother, she had to be hiding somewhere. What I felt for Carter was magical and everything seemed to be falling together perfectly. Add that to the way the girls had included me into their tribe, and I had to look down just to make sure that I wasn't about to slip in some fucking fairy dust and lose it all.

"Go. We need girl time." Stella stood and shooed her brother away. "And Sophie has a glow about her, I think that she needs to dish."

Carter leaned down and placed a quick but gentle kiss against my lips before giving a chin nod to rest of the girls. "Keep the chaos to a minimum."

"You are not spoiling our fun, now go." Stella pointed toward the door.

Carter gave me a wink and was gone.

"Before we get plastered, I think we really do need to

celebrate Piper's promotion by taking a moment to thank the Lord Almighty for his blessings," Ariel suggested.

I looked at her, not realizing that she was so religious. Ariel picked up her phone and dialed a number before turning it on speakerphone and setting it in the middle of the table.

"Hey, you redheaded stepchild, what are you doing calling Ringo on a Friday night?" Instantly recognizing the voice coming through the speaker and realizing that there must be some joke about prayers and Ringo.

"Why aren't you with that Greek God of yours? Oh wait, I'm with him," Ringo said with a laugh.

"Shut up, you are not. He's at home. But I do hope that you find your own Greek God. Anyway, I need a favor."

"Name it, and if I can make it happen, I will. If I can't, we'll see *who* I can do, I mean what I can do to make it happen."

I laughed at his intentional faux pas.

"I need a table Sunday for seven. We're celebrating."

"What are we celebrating?" he asked, including himself in the party.

"We are celebrating our friend Piper. She earned the position as the new motorcycle deputy for Orange County." Ariel shot me a devious smirk. "And you remember Sophia, right? Well, let's just say that she has been one lucky girl this week."

Ringo squealed. Honest to God squealed. "Please tell old Ringo that it is with that blond Adonis that couldn't keep his hands or his eyes off her that night. If not, does she happen to know where I can find him?"

"Sorry, Ringo, but yes that is him."

"Damn. Why are all the ones I want straight? Life just doesn't seem fair."

"Maybe you'll find a Greek God and Adonis and live happily ever after in debauchery."

"Oh, my goals in life have just expanded." Ringo let out a wistful sigh as if coming back down from the clouds. "Okay. So, we have two things to celebrate, I will have a table for you. Now, let me go and maybe I can find my own reason to celebrate." Right before he hung up, we heard him say, "Oh! Yoo-hoo, Mr. Sailorman, I was just talking about you."

"Oh my God, is he for real? I mean, I met him at the auction and thought he was hysterical, but this is too much. I love him." I could just imagine Ringo celebrating with Mr. Sailorman.

"Well, it looks like we are going to Bananas Sunday morning," Ariel said. "Do we want to ride?"

"I'd like to drive my car since it's the last day I'll have a cruiser. Who wants to pile in it?"

"That would be hysterical. A few of us ride and several could pile in the back of Piper's car like criminals." Stella's mind was already concocting some elaborate scheme.

"You're warped." I bumped Stella's shoulder. "But it would be funny. By the way, is anyone going to tell me what the hell Banana's is?"

"Oh. My. God." Stella could barely get the words out from laughing so hard. "Wait until you see this place. It is a drag show set in a fifties style diner during a church service."

"What?" That didn't even make sense to me.

"I couldn't make this shit up if I tried. The waitresses all wear outfits that resemble that old television show *Mel's Diner* with Alice and Flo. Of course, there's a redhead with a beehive hairdo running around snapping bubble gum, telling everyone to, 'kiss my grits.'"

"It's Ringo though; he makes the show," Ariel said smiling brightly about some fond memory. "He and the other performers are all in gospel choir robes singing old hymns. But pay close attention, he has a habit of changing the words."

I was cracking up, already picturing the image. Sunday was going to be a blast; it couldn't come quick enough for me.

"Soph, I'll swing by tomorrow and pick up your vest if you don't mind." Ariel gave me a devious smile.

"Okay."

"Since Banana's is now out of the way, dish," Ariel demanded staring at me.

"Spill." Stella banged her fist on the table.

I gave Stella a puzzled look. "You want to know about sex with your brother? I find so many things wrong with that."

"Like I fucking care, you can leave my brother's name out."

"I want to know if you've talked about what happened all of those years ago?" Leo brought our happy conversation to a halt.

"No, we didn't discuss the past. I don't know how. You guys don't get it . . ." I bit my lower lip and stared off, over their heads, and toward the other side of the bar.

"Has he asked?"

I took a second to ponder, realizing that aside from that first night at Sixes, he hasn't actually mentioned my leaving.

"He did, but we were both too angry to talk like rational adults."

"I understand not wanting to share with us . . . well, actually I don't because you should share everything with us, but that is something we can discuss a different day, but you should tell him." Stella tried to add her normal humor and still infuse her strength into me. I could sense that she supported me keeping this a secret until I told him.

"It's not that easy." I let out a sigh, the weight of ten years pressing on my shoulders. "You don't get it, none of you do. You have no clue what it's like to live a carefree life and then have the rug ripped out from under you." Slowly, my sorrow was leaking out and turning on them, and for some reason, I couldn't stop it. "No one gets it. No one understands what it's like to lose everything, to know that everyone else is happy and that you are stuck with the shit end of the stick." I was angry, not at them but at the situation.

"I get it, I totally understand," Vivian said in a near whisper. "My husband and I met our freshman year of high school and that was it. Our hearts just recognized each other, you know what I mean?"

I nodded because I totally knew what she meant. The first time Carter pulled me over, something in our hearts just recognized each other. I know that sounded corny but it was true.

"We got married a month after graduation, never regretted it, not once. He was . . ."

Was? Oh my God. What did she mean was?

She took a deep breath. "He was a deputy and last year he was killed. So, if you're going to tell us that no one understands what it feels like to know sunshine, only to then get thrust into the middle of a never-ending thunderstorm, then you are extremely naive."

Another wave of quietness passed over our table, but instead of being full of sympathy, it was full of heartbreak.

"Where are those drinks?" Stella spun around in her seat, avoiding eye contact with me.

"Here you go," the waitress said as she placed a tray full of shot glasses in the middle of our table. "You have Lemon Drops, Washington Apples, Woo Woos, and Stella's personal favorite, Blow Jobs. Give me a wave when you want more. I'll get some food sent over as well."

"We always start the night with Blow Jobs." Stella moved her glass to the edge of the table and then stood. "I love both of you, and honestly, I don't want to walk in either of your shoes. But the one thing that we are here for is to remind both of you that life goes on, and we are here to help you. So, everyone please stand. Here's to tough times and tougher women."

They all cheered and then leaned over and picked up the shot glass sans hands. I followed suit, and in one gulp, the drink was sliding down the back of my throat and my glass was popped back on to the table. Picking up a second glass, which must have been the Washington Apple, I downed it and then grabbed the yellow one, Lemon Drop.

"Hold on for a second," Leo said so she and everyone else could down their Washington Apples. "Take a breather for a second and then we will do the other two."

Tonight, I was determined to drown my sorrow beginning with these four shots.

"You know I'm used to being everyone's pitiful friend, I don't want their pity, never have." Vivian brought her face close to mine. "Don't you settle for it, either. From what I can see there isn't one thing wrong with you. Look at you, you're beautiful, you're healthy, you're whole."

I downed the fuckin' Lemon Drop and glared at her. "Fuck you." She didn't know anything about me, not one single thing. I wasn't whole. I raced off to find the bathroom.

Inside, I leaned over the basin and turned the cold water on to splash water on my face. Clutching the sides of the sink, I tried to regain my composure, I just needed to call someone to come get me. I looked up at the sound of the door swinging open and groaned at the sight of Vivian standing there.

"Come to finish the job?"

"Stop it, will you?"

She gripped my shoulders and jerked me upright, forcing me to stand in front of the mirror. "Look at yourself, you are beautiful."

"Not really, I'm not whole, you have no clue, no fucking clue what I've been through."

"You're right. I don't, and neither does anyone else because you won't let them in. If you want to keep your secret, that's fine, but you can't hold it over our heads for not understanding when you haven't given us a chance."

"He wants kids, I can't have them," I said as I wrapped my fingers around Vivian's wrist that rested on my shoulder. "Even when we're joking he talks about naming children. I can't do that to him."

"Who cares if you can't have kids? Who cares that you've been through some shit? The way I see it is that people like us have two options: be pitied or get stronger. Which one are you going to be?" She tapped my head. "You need to wake up and realize that there is a man that apparently has waited ten years to find you. I'm going to let you think about this." Vivian waved her hand in the air as if thoughts were floating around. "Sophie, I think you're strong but you're afraid. Ask yourself what is it that truly frightens you. When you know the answer, you'll be ready to move on with your life. When you're done in here come on out, we'll be waiting for you. And for what it's worth, I'm always here if you need someone to listen."

When the door closed, I slid down the wall, pulled my legs up, laid my head on my knees, and let the gut-wrenching sobs hit me. I expected someone to come running in at any moment, thinking that I was being slaughtered, but I couldn't stop. It hurt, everything hurt so fucking bad. I hated myself. I hated life. And most of all I hated that Vivian was right. I straightened my legs and pounded my fists against the floor as I continued to wail.

When there was nothing left to cry out, I wiped my nose, stood up, and looked at my face in the mirror. My nose resembled Rudolph's, my cheeks looked more like I was suffering from rosacea, and my eyes were in the middle of hay fever season. I snatched a paper towel and dampened it to clean away the mascara streaks and then sniffled some more, drying the last of my tears before pushing out of the bathroom door.

Back at the table, I picked up the last shot then downed it. "Let's dance." I was listening to the alcohol, which was telling me that I should dance as I spread my arms out, tilted my head up to the lights, and twirled as Rachel Platten sang "Fight Song." When the song was over, whether it was Vivian's words, the song, or that Carter Lang, the only guy that I'd ever fallen in love with was picking me up tonight, I was happier than I had been in a long time, and full of hope.

Walking . . . or was it wobbling, back to our table, Stella gave me a vibrant smile. "Feel better?"

I nodded.

"Ready for our drinking game?" she asked.

"What game?"

"We call it, Woulda, Coulda, Shoulda. It's sorta like Truth or Dare for alcoholics. Every sentence has to have a would you, could you, or should you, and involve drinking. Ariel can start."

"Would y'all go dance in front of everyone like a chicken with its head cut off?"

I glanced to the center of the table and noticed that two more shots for each of us and some food had been placed there.

"So, what happens if we're all willing to do it?" I asked, trying to understand if this was automatically a dare.

"We drink," Leo said, picking up a shot.

"And what if no one wants to do it?"

"We drink," Leo said as she twirled her glass.

"And if only a few did it am I to assume that we still drink?"

"You catch on quick." Leo handed me a shot glass.

We each downed one, and then ran, as fast as seven fairly

intoxicated women could run, to the dance floor. Laughing as the DJ played "Fight Like a Girl" by Bomshel. I jumped around in my version of an African tribal dance before moving with the others as Stella started doing the chicken dance, and just before the song ended, one of these drunk bitches—Vivian—got the bright idea to wrap her arm around my shoulders and pull me into the line to start a cancan. I cracked up laughing. Unfortunately, we looked nothing like the Rockettes. When the song finally ended, we headed back to our table.

Grabbing a slider from the basket, I ate and drank some water while we decided who went next.

"Sophie's new, let her have a go," Ariel said, nominating me.

I thought for a moment before saying, "Would you switch phones with someone and allow them to text anyone in your contact list?" Watching the stunned looks on some of their faces and a cackle coming from Stella and Vivian, I knew that I had hit on a genius idea. Everyone pulled out a phone, and I kept my eye on the one I wanted to grab. "Put them in the middle, and then we will all just grab one, just not your own. Make sure to unlock it." When we counted to three, I dove for the iPhone with the orange OtterBox with a bar and shield logo.

I wasn't overly worried about who got my phone. I didn't have many names in my contact list except family. I opened the phone and went to settings, moved the icon to block caller ID, and then scrolled through her contacts.

Nothing.

He wasn't in her phone.

Fine. That wouldn't stop me. I entered his number into her phone and then pulled up the text screen.

Unknown Caller: Do you know how fucking hot I find you? There is something about a rocket scientist's brain that fucking turns me on. Just thinking about you, your dark hair, and chocolate eyes makes me wet.

I watched as the three dots flashed across the screen.

Ian: Haha. Very funny. Who the fuck is this?

Unknown Caller: If I told you, I'd have to shoot you or ask your brother to shoot you.

Ian: Enough. Really, who is this?

Unknown Caller: I'm serious. I think that you are the sexiest man. But I know that you don't see me that way.

Ian: Are we in fucking high school?

Unknown Caller: Does that turn you on, Ian? Me, in a catholic school girl uniform. My skirt rising up as I bend over to pick up my books?

"Sophie has an entire conversation going. Who the hell are you texting?" Stella leaned over my shoulder to read what I was typing and snorted. "Oh shit, that's good. Keep going."

"Fuck, that's my phone." Leo tried to pull it from my hands, but I swatted her away.

"Stop. Let me finish."

Ian: Please tell me that you're over eighteen?

Unknown Caller: I am legal. But I also want to do things with you that are illegal in several states, maybe even some countries.

Ian: Oh God.

Unknown Caller: Actually, you will shout: Oh God, oh God, oh God!!!

Ian: Okay, who is this?

Unknown Caller: Good night, gorgeous.

Ian: Oh, no you don't. Don't stop texting until you tell me your name.

Ian: You still there?

Ian: I will figure out who the fuck this is.

I returned Leo's caller ID to its normal setting and

handed back her phone. I watched as she read the text conversation and threw her head on the table.

"No, no, no. He thinks I'm a lesbian."

"Don't worry. I turned off your caller ID before I texted him. I turned it back on when I was done. So, don't text again, otherwise he will have your number," I told her. "Wait. Why does he think you're a lesbian?"

"I don't know, just comments he has made over the years, and I get so tongue-tied around him that I can't say anything to correct him."

Stella and I leaned closer together and stared at Leo.

"No. Whatever you two are thinking about, the answer is no." Leo waved her index finger between the two of us.

We let out a laugh and then grabbed our phones back. Whoever had my phone had been having a rather interesting conversation with Carter.

Me: Hey, gorgeous, I've been thinking about you all night.

Carter: What about?

Me: About your big cock.

Carter: What?

"Oh shit, who had my phone?"

"I did." Vivian waved her hand as she read her own phone's texts.

Me: The girls wanted to know about you as a lover. So, I told them you were incredible and that you promised to drunk fuck me tonight.

Carter: Is that what you want?

Me: I always want you to fuck me, drunk or not.

Carter: When?

Me: What time are you coming to get me?

Carter: Now.

Me: Ride the motorcycle.

Carter: Why?

Me: So, I can have the roar of the engine between my legs and the roar of your engine inside me.

Carter: What? You want sex on the bike?

Me: Yes. Doesn't that sound hot?

Carter: That sounds fucking hot. I'm on my way.

Me: Good because I'll be sitting here getting wet just thinking about your big cock.

"Holy shit, Vivian, you should write porn screenplays." Stella shouted, and the entire bar silenced. "Sorry." Stella gave a slight wave. "You didn't write a lot of words, you just got right to the action. A part of me wants me to seek mental help because what you wrote is hot and it's to my brother."

"Raise your hand if you think the phone game is our new go-to girls' night out game?" Ariel held her hand up, waiting for everyone else to join her. When we did, she smiled. "Perfect. That's our game until someone can come up with something more fun."

We all fixed plates, grabbing a little of everything from the baskets of food in the center of the table. I reached for the last shot while everyone else grabbed theirs. "Thank you for welcoming me to my first official girls' night." We drank the butterscotch flavored drink. "Was that our fifth?"

"It was your sixth." A warm familiar male voice said from behind me.

"Shit," I shouted like it was bingo and I had just won. "You scared me."

"Did you ride the bike up?" Ariel asked.

I looked at Carter and saw him raise one eyebrow. "No."

"You didn't? Why not?" Leo jumped in.

"Because, although that text was hot, it didn't sound like Sophie, so I figured one of you had gotten your hands on her phone."

Our laughs stopped at the sound of male voices coming near us.

"Okay, what's going on?" Kayson asked.

"Did you get text messages?" Carter asked, a low chuckle in his voice.

"Yep," Ian commented, coming to stand next to Kayson.

"And me." Tristan smirked at Stella.

Wow, three of my cousins got texted, I needed to grab Stella's phone and see what was sent to him.

"So, what's going on?" Kayson stood behind Ariel. "Ian called me and told me that he had just received the strangest text. So, I called Tristan and Damon. It seems that Damon was the only one left out of the prank. I'm assuming that you are all drunk texting?"

"Mine didn't sound drunk and whoever texted me blocked their caller ID." Ian waved his phone out for us all to see.

"Mine wasn't blocked, but it didn't sound like Stella, either. It was much too tame." Tristan stepped up and tugged on Stella's braid.

I bit my lip, holding back my smile.

Carter's warm breath tickled against the back of my neck. "What did I tell you about biting that lip?" His voice was low so only I could hear. "Let's go home."

"You're no fun."

"Nice diversion," Stella whispered, unfortunately we were drunk and in a bar, so our voices were louder than normal and the guys all stopped to stare. "Shit."

"We'll figure it out." Carter picked me up in a fireman's hold and carried me out the door.

Chapter Thirteen

CARTER

*E*ven hammered, she was adorable. I knew by the text that it wasn't her and if she was as drunk as the message claimed, then I wasn't relying on her to stay seated on a motorcycle so I had driven my Jeep. I groaned as I drove and looked down at my crotch, apologizing to him that there wouldn't be any sex tonight drunk or otherwise. Truth be told, I was just happy to hold her while we slept—

Holy fuck, who was I? This wasn't me. I was a wrap it, tap it, and go kind of guy. She'd been back less than a month, and I already saw my future with her. A future I wanted. I reminded myself that I had an appointment with the attorney next week and all of the shit would get taken care of.

Pulling into her driveway, I reached into my pocket and pulled out a copy of her house key that I had snagged from her kitchen drawer earlier that day. Walking around to the passenger door, I opened it and caught her just as she attempted to leap into my arms.

"Careful, princess, or we'll both go toppling backward."

"That'd be fun. Carter, you know what?" She tapped my cheek a little harder than I was sure she had intended.

"What?" I asked as she leaned against me, not moving a bit.

"I want you to fuck me. Did you hear me? I said that I want you to FUCK ME."

"Yes, I heard you. Let's go inside because I'm sure that your neighbors heard you as well."

"That's okay, my neighbors are all family." She waved her hand, dismissing my comment.

"I know, that's what concerns me. I'd rather not have five angry Greek men cornering me or your furious Greek mom giving me that damn evil eye."

Helping her walk up to her door, I unlocked it while I tried to hold her upright, but she kept sliding her hands into the back of my jeans. "Soph, stop. Let me get you upstairs."

Her mischievous grin somehow had my dick hardening, and I knew that it was going to be a long, long night.

Once I finally got her upstairs, I set her on the bed and then turned to dig around in her dresser drawer to try to find her sleep shirt. Pulling one out, I turned back around to undress her, but she had already removed her top. I stopped dead in my tracks.

She brought her index finger up and flicked her nipple. "No feeling, none. Fake. That is why you don't need to suck on them, no feeling."

My God, my Sophie, what happened to you?

Moving to her, I sat on the side of the bed and held her face between my palms.

"Sophie, what happened?" My eyes burned as I fought back the tears wanting to fall. Slowly, I let my hands slide down, just barely tracing the scars that stretched across the center of each of her breasts.

I expected her to pull away or smack my hands, but she didn't. She just took shallow breaths and whispered, "I went to the doctor to get a prescription for birth control, and he did a blood test since it was close to my annual physical anyway. My results came back, and it said I had cancer, it was breast cancer." She sat up and grabbed ahold of the front of my shirt and shook. "I had breast cancer. I couldn't stay, my mom was in California. I didn't start college that fall. Cancer. Motherfucking cancer."

My head was spinning as I tried to take in everything that she was telling me. She threw herself back on to the bed and yanked at the button of her jeans, growing more and more frustrated with each tug. Gently, I moved my hands to cover hers, she was getting frustrated, I needed to do something, "Let me do that."

Her hands fell to the mattress as I flicked the button open and started working the jeans down her legs. When she spoke again, her voice was tiny almost child-like.

"I got to California, and my mom, she was already there, she took me to a radiologist. Carter, are you listening? Breast cancer, I was stage three. It was called triple negative. I didn't know what that meant at the time, but I sure as fuck found out. Carter, I didn't want to leave, I promise, I didn't. I was in love with you. I was getting on the pill so we could. . ."

All of the anger that I had spewed at the beginning of our reunion, the ten years of loathing I had allowed to fester inside me, seemed to boil away, leaving me feeling like a major asshole. Sophie, my Sophie, was trying to keep her shit together on the other side of the country, and I was feeding anger. She was eighteen and faced breast cancer and that truth made my own heartache seem so insignificant.

"Triple negative isn't good, it's bad, really bad. It's aggressive and invasive and has a high chance of coming back. That was why I was gone so long. They kept a close eye on me for almost five years after I entered remission. I felt like every other month I was having surgery, I went through chemo for-fuckin'-ever and the radiation was the worse."

I'd finally gotten her jeans off her and helped her slide up the bed. She patted her back.

"You saw my tattoo. It covers the burn marks from the radiation."

Leaning forward, running my fingers along the curve of her breasts, kissing each scar that I came across, pockmarks, burn scars, small and large incision scars.

"I've been through hell, Carter, but the worst part was cutting you out of my life." Sophie grabbed a pillow, slid down, and curled into it as if she could protect herself with feathers and cotton. She continued talking, but her words had faded to more of a mumble, I listened for a few minutes before peeling myself away just long enough to run down-stairs, lock the door, and grab her water and some Tylenol.

Before crawling in to bed, I put everything on her night-stand and then got under the covers and pulled her into me to cradle her all night. I fell asleep holding this beautiful tall woman who seemed so tiny and fragile in my arms.

I woke at the sound of a groan. Jumping out of bed, I moved to the side of her bed and snagged one of the bottles of water, holding it out for her to sip. Then dumped two Tylenols into my hand and held them out to her.

"What is that?"

"It's Tylenol. It will help the headache."

She pushed my hand away as she darted from the bed and flew into the bathroom, the retching sounds reached me before I got to her. She was throwing up. Turning on her sink, I let the water run to warm up and then slid a washcloth underneath, wrung it out, and then handed it to her. That was when it hit her that she was naked. Throwing her arms around her chest, she curled up into a tight ball.

"Get out. Get out, get out. I need a shirt."

"Soph, stop. Don't hide, please."

"Carter, just go."

"Sophie, I'm not going." I waited until her stomach was empty and the dry heaves had passed before I bent and lifted her up. When she wouldn't look at me, I lowered my head and placed fervent kisses over each breast and collarbone, under her chin, and then on her cheeks. Turning her around so that she faced her vanity mirror with me behind her, I brushed her hair to the side.

She crossed her arms to cover her chest, but I just unfolded them and held them to her sides.

"Don't believe the mirror—believe me. I'm the one that is in love with you. You're beautiful. Believe me, I've been in love with you for ten years."

She dropped her chin to her chest and mumbled, "Can you give me a second?"

"Sure, princess. But please don't hide from me ever again. When you're done just come out here and let me hold you. It's best if you just sleep off your hangover anyway." I handed her the bottle of water and the Tylenol, then kissed the side of her head before leaving.

While I waited for her to come out, I ran downstairs and fixed myself a cup of coffee and grabbed my iPad and headphones. When I came back into her room, she was curled up in bed, with a shirt on, facing away from me.

"Next time they invite me to girls' night out, remind me to say no."

I chuckled. "I don't think they held you down and forced the drinks down your throat." I laid my iPad on the nightstand.

"Shut up. It was peer pressure, and I blame it all on your sister." She moved her head to my lap, and the muscles in my stomach clenched, while I willed my dick to behave.

"Carter?"

"Yes?"

"When we were in the bathroom . . ."

I let out a low chuckle, I was wondering if she had picked up on what I had said.

"Never mind."

Sliding the hair away from her face, I looked down at her smooth skin. For the first time, I really noticed the hint of dark circles under her eyes. After Googling about breast cancer and chemotherapy this morning on my phone while she slept, I had learned that dark circles were one of many side effects. Changes in hair texture was another one, which explained why her hair was straight compared to the wavy curls she had when she was a teenager. "Yes, I told you that I love you, I have for ten years."

"I've never stopped loving you, either." Her words were more of a moan than a declaration as she rubbed her cheek against my lap like a kitten and got comfortable before falling back to sleep.

I thought back to when she got sick earlier and hated the thought that I wasn't there for her when she was going through chemotherapy and all the times she must have been sick. Part of me hated the fact that she refused me the opportunity to help her but in the long run it all worked out. I needed to focus on that and stop feeling cheated.

She rested quietly until her stomach let out a gurgle, causing her to wake.

"You hungry?"

"Uh-huh."

Helping her out of bed, we headed downstairs. I searched for something to make, but her cabinets were pretty bare.

"Cereal?" I asked since all I could find was Peanut Butter Cap'n Crunch, grabbing the milk from the fridge I set it in front of her and then moved to get a bowl and a spoon.

"Will you also get the Hershey's Syrup?" She pointed to her pantry cabinet.

I opened it and found several boxes of cereal and several

bottles of syrup. Shaking my head at the realization that Sophie had an addiction problem, I couldn't help but laugh. Well, at least breakfast in bed would be easy. I grabbed a glass, so she could make chocolate milk and was shocked when she swirled the syrup on top of her cereal.

"Something about that is gross and at the same time makes me want Reese's Peanut Butter Cups."

"I know, right? They have Reese's cereal, but it tastes like cardboard." She took a mouthful and chomped, the crunching sound echoing in the silent kitchen. "Please tell me that we're taking it easy today, I don't know if my head can handle anything else."

"Whatever you want to do."

"If the sound doesn't kill me, can we practice my mad motorcycle skills?"

"Of course. Can we also talk?" Sophie's shoulders slumped and I hated putting this pressure on her but I wasn't going to let her hide or run, not again. Sitting in the chair across from her, I reached for her hand. "Do you realize that we have only been back together a week and can you truly tell me that you could walk away again?"

"But this time is different."

"Soph, look at me. We may have not had sex on the hood of the car the night of your eighteenth birthday but you and I both know that I made you come. You shouted my name and I never forgot the taste of you."

"Carter, you saw me, do you understand everything?"

"No. I want you to tell me."

"I can't give you children."

"We can adopt."

"The cancer may return."

"So? Everyone has the chance of having cancer."

"I don't look normal."

"Well, let's be honest, you've never acted normal, either."

Standing I went around the table and knelt in front of her. "I'm not going anywhere."

When she wrapped her arms around me, I stood and held her close, feeling her tighten her legs around my waist. She was still only wearing a shirt. Lowering my waistband, I slid her down until I was buried deep inside her.

"Carter."

"Hold on, baby." Walking into the living room, I sat on the couch and settled back. Brushing my fingers under her shirt, I slowly moved my hands up until I was cupping her breasts. "Please, princess, I need to see you, all of you. Please give me all of you."

Sophie rose up on one leg to balance herself as she pulled her shirt off, and I let out a groan as she slid back down onto my cock. She was gorgeous, and I knew that this was going to be all about her and showing her how fucking sexy I found her.

"Sophie, I'm in love with you. I don't think I've ever not been in love with you. But seeing you, having you here, God, I can't take my eyes off you, you're so fucking gorgeous."

I held her hips and lifted her, moving her up and down. When she slid her tongue into my mouth, it wasn't a kiss, it was pure passion. I was wild for her, needed to feel her, see her come. Pinching her clit between my thumb and forefinger, I massaged gently, watching her eyes darken with her desire as she rode me. Her tight body stroking my cock, driving me wilder and crazier as I fought back every urge to come as I watched my Sophie, the real Sophie, no mask, bare, letting me have all of her. My free hand slid up and down her back, pulling her closer to me so my face was right where her skin had been stretched to form new breasts, and I rubbed my face over her pale soft skin, not to mark or claim, but to soothe. "Do you know how fucking sexy you are? Do you feel me, this is what you do to me, you, Sophie, and this perfect body of yours."

I trailed kisses along each breast and licked the scars, I wasn't sure if she had any feeling but I did and at that moment all I wanted to do was to taste her tits.

"Carter, I'm coming. I'm gonna come."

With Sophie's words, I was right behind her. I poured myself inside of her making a silent promise that I was going to get some things in order so I could make Sophie mine forever.

Chapter Fourteen

SOPHIE

*A*t first, waking up curled against a man had been foreign to me, but I was quickly learning to like it, and knowing that there were no secrets between us gave me a new outlook. I couldn't believe that in less than a month, I had my own home, friends, and I was opening up to the man I'd always fantasized about having a future with.

Sitting up, Carter snaked his hand around my chest and pulled me back down and under him. Braced over me, he moved a hand to wipe my bangs off my forehead.

"Have fun today. I'm going up to the community center this morning then I'll run by my condo and grab my uniform and switch out my bike. I'm back on shift tomorrow."

He released me, and I missed the feel of heat from his body as I slid from bed. I headed into the bathroom to shower and get ready, then dressed in what the girls called "official Iron Orchids gear" of jeans and boots. I didn't have the vest yet, but Ariel promised she'd have it back soon.

Going downstairs, I smiled at the sight of Carter in my kitchen, standing in front of the coffee maker.

"Morning princess, you look beautiful."

I shifted my weight from side to side, debating whether he could tell that between my thighs was tingling. He stirred my insides when he swept the pad of his thumb against my lower lip.

My front door flew open and Ariel's and Stella's voices filled my house as I gave Carter a wide-eyed look.

"I unlocked it." He lifted a brow and gave me a quick kiss. "Morning, ladies."

Their smiles said it all—they were happy to see him there.

"Here you go." Ariel thrust my vest into my hands. "It's official, you're one of us."

"I'm part of the gang?"

"Fuck, not you, too?"

I looked at Stella and gave her a high five. When the sound of more motorcycles rumbled up my drive, I turned and headed back over to Carter. "I don't know how long this is today, but . . ."

"No worries, have fun."

Trying to keep the girls from hearing, I turned my head away from them. "Was the week everything you wanted?"

"Nooo." He gave me a wide grin. "It was more." Carter set his coffee on the counter behind him and then took a step closer, wrapped his hands around my waist, and pulled me in to him. "You and me, I like this shit." I couldn't help but smile. Others might not find that romantic, but I found it romantic as hell.

"Soph, let's go." Stella snapped her fingers.

Carter's warm hands lightly squeezed my shoulders as he turned me around and swatted my ass before sending me out to the girls. "Have fun. Don't get arrested."

"You are not ruining my fun," I hollered back at him as I followed the girls out my front door.

Everly and Vivian were riding separately since they lived in the opposite direction and could head home after breakfast instead of coming back to my place, which left Piper, Leo, Stella, and me to ride in the cruiser. Ariel jumped in the front seat before any of us could say anything, which left Leo, Stella, and me crawling into the back.

"So, how big is your house? From the outside it looks huge," Piper said.

"It's enormous. Five bedrooms, remember I'm Greek and we are supposed to have big families."

"But aren't you an only child? That doesn't scream large family to me."

"Yes, but my parents were madly in love. My *bampas*—"

"Your what?" Piper asked.

"Sorry, *Bampas* is Greek for dad."

"Kayson calls his mom Mana, but he doesn't call his dad that," Ariel said, trying to get clarity.

"Kayson's dad and my mom are siblings, they were born here and are more Americanized. His mana and my father were both born in Greece, so it's different."

"Where is your father now?" Piper asked, wanting to understand the size of Greek families.

"He died when I was five from pancreatic cancer."

"And your mom never remarried?"

"Nope. I don't think she's even dated. She is happy and just waiting until the day they are together again."

"Oh, that is so sad and yet so beautiful." Ariel sighed.

"We're getting way too serious," Stella quipped.

I appreciated the diversion. "Now, about joining Iron Orchids, do I have to go through a prospect phase or anything like performing a ritual that requires I bite off the head of a bat?"

Stella let out a loud laugh. "I think we'll leave biting off a bat's heads to Ozzy Osbourne. But, you know, we never even thought about initiation shit. I could have a lot of fun with this."

"Maybe I don't want to join you after all."

Everyone let out a laugh as the car slowed, and I turned to see people move out of the way staring at the cruiser with women in the backseat and its escort of biker women. Moving my hand to open the door, I realized for the first time that there was no latch. Holy shit.

"How do we get out?" I asked as Piper laughed. She got out of her car and stood outside my window, peering in with a wide smile as she held up her cell phone to snap a photo. She was saying something to Ariel when Everly and Vivian joined her and they pointed at the three of us. I was positive that they were discussing who all to send the photo to.

"Oh, hell to the no," I said.

"Silly girls, they've forgotten who they're dealing with," Stella whispered. "When we get out, keep your hands together and behind your back like you're handcuffed. The crowd won't know. Then follow my lead."

I gave Leo a weary smile, and she shrugged. "In for a penny, in for a pound."

There were a few more minutes of fun at our expense before Piper finally decided to open the door. "At least we know that none of you've been arrested before. Otherwise, you would've realized that you can't get out of the backseat of a sheriff's car. Now, come on you hardened criminals, let's eat."

Turning my legs out so that I could stand and still keep my hands behind my back, I got out first, Leo and Stella following. All three of us were quiet.

"What are you three up to?" Piper asked, showing her first sign of concern.

"You're not getting us," Stella screamed and ran.

"Take that, pig," I shouted and followed Stella.

Leo didn't say anything as she followed us, but her laughter rang out between screams of horror from people trying to get away from the escaping convicts. When Stella neared the door, she righted herself, and the three of us went in. Other patrons stared at us in bewilderment.

"Y'all are fucking nuts," Ariel said as she entered the restaurant with the other girls. "Stella was hard to handle before, but I have a feeling that we just doubled the trouble. And Leo? You went along with this?"

Leo smiled and shrugged. "I have my BFF back, she was always a bad influence on me. Who do you think would bring me an outfit every day to put on so that I didn't have to walk around school in an ankle-length skirt and long-sleeve shirt? I mean, this is Florida. I had an entire wardrobe at her house. Sophie kept me as normal as I could be." Leo turned and gave me a fist bump.

"Is that Miss Seven Hundred And Fifty Dollars A Night herself?" Ringo hollered from the stage, leaving me to hide behind my hands at the mere implication that I was a prostitute. Stella let out a loud guffaw.

"Let me just sprinkle you with some holy water." He spritzed some water in my face. "No worries, it is from the garden of Evian. I'm glad you are here. I was just about to debut my latest rendition of a timeless treasure. I was inspired Friday night." Ringo winked.

"Mr. Sailorman?" I asked.

"Oh, darling, don't you know it. When the song hit me? All I can say is . . . it was orgasmic."

Ringo kept talking as we found our way to our table. When we were seated and he started singing, Ariel was the first to catch on.

"Holy shit, do you hear this?"

I listened closer to the words, recognized it as a church hymnal but being Greek Orthodox it wasn't a song we sang. As I paid closer attention to the words I threw my head on the table and banged my forehead.

"Oh my God, he is so going to hell for this one," I said between my gales of laughter.

"At least we will know where to find him," Stella quipped.

Ringo's gorgeous countertenor voice was what masked the words he was actually singing.

"Burst forth!" The crowd laughed as Ringo made hand gestures. "He is risen, he is risen." Ringo's smiling face and raised brows forewarned us that something major was coming . . . hopefully, not literally. "A triumphant lay," he sang.

By the time the song ended, I had tears streaming down my face. I joined in with the others shouting, "Amen."

Only to be singled out by Ringo and taught the ways-of-the-gays. "Oh no sweetie, it's not that type of church. We do a different kind of worshiping when we're on our knees." He gave a guy in the audience an overly exaggerated wink.

Catching on rather quickly, I listened to those around me and corrected my praise. "Hey men." When the shouts died down, and we returned to our seats I turned to Leo and asked, "Does that song 'He's Risen' really contain the phrases 'bursting forth' and 'a triumphant lay'?" Since she was raised in a strict Pentecostal home, I figured if anyone would know, it would be her.

"Unfortunately, yes. But not in that order and definitely not the same meaning." Leo shook her head.

We finished our breakfast and toasted to Piper's new position as the first female motorcycle deputy for Orange County.

Ringo's next song was a dedication to Piper, he sang "If My Sister's in Trouble" from *Sister Act*.

"I need a favor." Everyone stared at me as if I had just announced that I was an alien. "I have an idea for a new book series, and I definitely need Piper and Leo's help, but maybe the rest of you know someone that you can connect me with."

"Okay, what is it?" Leo asked. "You know that I'll do whatever I can."

"I admire the two of you so much and that your jobs are what most people think of as 'guy jobs.' I was intrigued by the idea of a book about women who work in a man's world. I want to shadow you and show how you manage and not just keep up but excel in predominately male stereotypical jobs. I want to inspire young girls to want to grow up to be mechanics and motorcycle deputies."

"I'm in. Tuesday is our slowest day; do you want to come in then? I'll tell my boss. He won't care." Leo grabbed her phone to send a text.

"I have to clear it with my chain of command, but I'll check into it immediately. How about Everly? She's a fire fighter."

"Shit, Everly, I didn't even think about that. I thought of you as a medic."

"I am a paramedic, I don't know about other places but here we all take EMT classes before we take fire standards. Once we're hired on by a fire department, we can opt to take classes such as paramedic training, hazardous material, water rescue, or even medevac, which gives us a raise in salary. I was a firefighter for a few years before I became a paramedic."

"I had no idea. You're the best. Will you check to see if I can come spend a day with you? Of course, with all of this I'll have enough to sell my editor on the idea. If she likes it and they make an offer, we will celebrate, my treat."

"Well, while we are all here." Stella gave me a devious smile. "Soph, we need to plan something. Did you know that tomorrow is Carter's birthday? He'll be thirty-one. He didn't want me to say anything, but we all know how well that works."

"He seriously thought you'd listen?"

"I know, right." Her grin got wider. "We need to do something epic. He's working tomorrow, and I'm assuming he will want to be with you in the evening, so it needs to happen during his shift. Any ideas?"

Everyone tossed out ideas, but since Piper, Everly, and Vivian all had to work tomorrow, that left Ariel and Leo to help Stella and me.

The last birthday Carter and I were together, he gave me a charm for the bracelet I had on. He'd actually had the pin he received when he graduated from the academy turned into a charm, and it still dangled there. When he had given it to me, I'd almost refused it, but after I left for California, I was so glad I hadn't.

Rubbing my fingers across its smooth surface, which at one time had been rough before I had turned it into my worry stone, I couldn't hold back the happy memories that we had shared, the nights that we had counted down until I was eighteen. With him being a sheriff and me not a legal adult, he fought so hard to not move our relationship too far, but God, the things we did to tide ourselves over. Studying the polish on my silverware, I tried not to look at anyone in the face to give my cheeks time to cool back down.

"Yeah . . . I agree, it needs to be epic," I finally said.

Chapter Fifteen

SOPHIE

*C*arter left my house just before six, and I headed into my office to make a list, search ideas for a birthday present, and get a little writing done before stores opened. Just before nine, I pulled into the mall parking lot and headed for Bloomingdales. I leaned over the counter in the cosmetic area and alternated between sniffing samples of colognes and then cans of coffee beans to clear my nose. I wasn't sure if I was trying to find his scent or one that would remind me of him, which was probably why I didn't just call his sister Stella. When I lifted the cap off the dark blue bottle of Amouage and spritzed the stick, images of Carter smiling at me as he leaned into my car window ruffled some distant memory. This was it. Not what he wore, but it was a scent that if I ever smelled it again, would remind me of my Carter. I swiped my credit card and signed the pad while the sales clerk wrapped the gift. The cologne was pricey, but it was just money, right?

Bampas had made sure that mom and I were taken care of after he was gone. He had owned a concrete business and had worked in tandem with Uncle George, who had taken over the business once *Bampas* passed. To this day, once a month, money from the company was deposited into Mom's account and mine. I had never spent a penny, my mom had a great job and I was making good money as an author. It was about time I spent some, and in the last few days, I had done just that, but what I had spent barely put a dent in it. I made a mental note to call my accountant about the check that I had written to Harley Davidson, lest she panic and think my account had been compromised.

Leaving the mall, I headed for Publix to get the stuff on my shopping list to make him a nice Greek dinner. I actually had no idea if he liked Greek food, but I crossed my fingers that he did. It was about all I could cook. I had decided to fry *loukoumades* for dessert since they were fast and he could put whatever he wanted on them, and hell, who didn't like homemade doughnuts? But my specialty was lamb and potatoes with homemade *tzatziki* sauce.

I had just enough time to put the groceries away and was changing my shirt when the chime of the bell from my door rang. I ran down the steps to greet the girls, buttoning my shirt each step of the way.

They walked in my house and kept going straight through to the garage and piled into my Countryman since I was driving. I headed out to the main road while Leo entered the address into my GPS for Fairvilla, a large adult entertainment store about thirty minutes away.

"Are you sure about this?" I asked as we pulled into the parking lot. "I think this is fucking hysterical, but will he? Will he get in trouble?"

"Don't worry. Piper has it all worked out," Stella assured me.

We walked inside the giant two-story building, and I was in awe. I had never been in a sex toy store this large . . . well, I'd never been in a sex store at all.

I turned at the sound of Ariel's laugh. She and Stella were holding up vibrators and comparing their assets, so to speak.

"I don't think I'd like that one." I pointed at a rather realistic looking one.

Stella held it close and petted it as if my words had insulted it. "Why ever not? This is the Chubby Fun."

"Something tells me it might feel more like giving birth than pleasure."

She let out a laugh. "Don't you know that all men have eight-inch dicks that are nearly six inches in girth, just go on Tinder and ask."

"And most are purple or pink," Ariel said, holding up two neon-colored vibrators.

"Actually, I've only seen one or two eight-inch penises and I'm a nurse. Don't believe a word of what men say, they don't know how to use a measuring tape," Stella crooned as she dragged me over to another area. She held a basket and tossed in bottles and jars.

"What's all that?"

"Lube, anal eze, flavored oils, body chocolate . . ." She dropped in item after item.

I looked at her, stunned, not because of body chocolate or lube but because of the thought of entry up the Hershey highway—no thank you. I clenched my butt cheeks just thinking about it.

Leo and Ariel were picking up things as well. As they came to stop next to us, Leo dropped her stuff into Stella's basket and Ariel dropped a few things in but kept the rest.

"Do you always contribute to Stella's depravity?"

They only smiled.

"Okay, let's get Carter's gift." I headed off to a row marked Inflatables. Holding up a black circle that read "Backdoor Blaster'" I shook my head and put it back down. Someone needed to talk with their marketing department about names. I mean, come on, what part of backdoor blaster sounded sexually appealing? Maybe call it the Great Beyond or Cum-a-Knockin'. Okay, I wasn't quitting my day job anytime soon, but the names of these toys were horrible.

I perused the shelves, scanning past a blow-up Tiffany doll, a Justin doll . . .

"Here it is," I said and held up one life-sized, inflatable sheep and tried not to consider why such a thing was even created. Heading to the cash register, I pulled out my card just as their front door chimed opened, and a lady that I recognized strolled in. "Holy shit, I know her, she's from my church. I've known her since I was born." Ducking behind the counter, I hid. "Oh my God, what if she tells people that she saw me here buying a blow-up sheep?" I crawled on my hands and knees around the side and hid under a rack of clothes.

"Soph . . ." Stella said my name louder than a whisper.

"Shut up." I crawled deeper into the rack, knocking some garments—if I could call them that—to the ground.

"Soph . . ."

"Will you shut up? She is such a gossip," I hissed out and crawled out of the rack into another taller one that held floor-length something or another.

"Soph, you do realize that she is in here as well?" Stella asked in all seriousness. "She can't say anything without condemning herself."

"Fuck. Why do you have to be so logical?" I stood and my hair was caught on something. A hard tug later, and I was free but my scalp hurt. "What is this stuff, anyway?" I gestured to the shiny black outfits.

"Dominatrix outfits. Want one?" Stella grabbed one and held it out to me.

"Nooo." I threw my hands out, trying to push it away.

"How about these?" Stella held up several pairs of panties

and showed how the crotch opened. "That was the first rack you hid in."

"Get out of my way." I let out a huff but was really only trying to contain my laugh as I walked back to the counter and took my sheep from the sales clerk.

Leo and I waited to the side while Stella and Ariel were rung up, turning to Ariel, "I don't want to know what you bought, don't tell me, don't talk about it." Ariel let out a laugh as I continued. "No. Don't go there. He's my cousin, and I don't want to hear about the two of you being all kinky and shit." She laughed louder and dangled a blindfold and what appeared to be a feather duster. "Cobwebs?"

"Shut up," she said and smacked my arm before we headed out and piled back into my car.

Stella took the sheep from me and sat in the backseat and started blowing. I constantly checked my rearview mirror as the thing got bigger and the number of cars that slowed down to see exactly what was going on inside my vehicle got higher and higher. Stella handed the sheep over to Ariel, who took over blowing it up.

"You guys do realize that you are giving a sheep a blow job, right?"

My seatback jerked as Stella smacked it.

"Truthfully, though, I think Leo needs to take a photo of this. You never know when this shit will come in handy for blackmail material." I turned to stare at Leo, but she wasn't moving. Glancing back at Stella in the rearview mirror, I saw a wide smile on her face.

"Oh, young grasshopper Sophie, you need to learn from the wise one. I don't give a fuck, and I already have just that kind of material on all of them. But nice try, I like your initiative."

I stuck out my tongue and laughed.

By the time we reached the sheriff's station, the sheep

was taking up the entire back seat, Ariel and Stella were squashed, and my MINI Countryman smelled of latex.

Opening the door, Stella uncurled from my backseat and made a call. I'm assuming whomever she was talking to was Piper's contact.

"Hi, Bridget, we're here . . . Yeah, the side entrance . . . Okay, coming up now." Stella pressed end call and slid her phone into her back pocket. "Got the ribbon?" she asked Ariel.

"Yep, right here." Ariel pulled out a giant roll of red ribbon, a pair of scissors, and some Scotch tape from her purse.

"Holy fuck, what all do you keep in that thing?" I grabbed the handle and peered in to what appeared to be the black hole.

We walked up a ramp, Stella carrying the sheep, which was almost life size, Ariel carrying her purse of magic tricks, and Leo staying a few steps behind, trying not to laugh at the two of them. A beautiful young woman with fiery red hair and a spattering of freckles opened the door.

"Holy Mother of Mary," she proclaimed. "What are you four up to?"

"It's Carter's birthday," I said as if that was explanation enough. Holding out my hand, I introduced myself. "Hi, I'm Sophie."

Her smile only got wider. "I know who you are. I was at the auction. My brother walked you across the stage."

"He was so sweet. He calmed me down. I was ready to run off stage and tell Ariel to fuck off."

Bridget let out a giggle and led us to a side room. "Okay, you'll see his name. You can only put stuff in his mailbox. It's used for inner office stuff."

We quickly moved. Ariel tied the ribbon around the sheep's neck, I grabbed the end and taped it to the inside of

Carter's box, and Stella set the sheep up nice and tall right in front, so everyone had to notice her.

"Now all we need you to do is to call Carter and tell him that before he gets off shift he needs to come by the station and pick up something that was delivered," Stella explained. "And if you want to make a few calls to his radio, we won't stop you. But remember to use your best sheep impersonation."

Bridget nodded, and we headed back out.

On the way out, I flipped off my caller ID and dialed Carter.

"Deputy Lang."

Fighting the urge to laugh, I pulled myself together and baaa-ed like a sheep before promptly hanging up.

About ten minutes later, Stella called him.

"Deputy Lang."

"Cahh-tahh."

"Who is this?"

Disconnect.

As we pulled up into my driveway, Leo opened her phone and sent a text with the picture of a sheep and a voice recording, "Cahh-tahh."

As the girls made themselves comfortable, I started the lamb, and they continued tormenting Carter.

"Do you see the irony here?" Leo pointed to me preparing dinner.

"No. What?"

"You're cooking lamb."

I groaned, afraid that Carter would assume I was taking the joke a little too far.

"Motherfucker." We all stopped to stare at Stella's outburst.

"What?" I asked.

"Blocked calls are now going straight to voice mail. Oh, he

isn't getting away that easily. We'll get Piper in on it." She texted Piper to let her know that we needed help.

I made a mental note not to let Stella know my birthday and to never piss her off.

The girls sat around my kitchen bar while I was getting stuff ready for dinner.

"How is everything going between the two of you? Looks like it's going well." Ariel pointed to my face. "You're smiling a lot more."

Before I had time to answer, Stella's phone rang. "It's Piper." She pressed speaker and we listened.

"Holy shit. I called a few of the guys, and now they are subtly adding sheep sounds over the radio. It reminds me of that movie *Super Troopers* when they did the meow shit. No one is saying 'copy' they're saying 'cahhh-py'. He called in to dispatch and Bridget answered with, 'Orange County Cahhh-pies'. I think he is ready to blow."

"That sounds like it might benefit Sophie then." Stella raised an eyebrow.

I shook my head, laughing.

"TMI," Piper said. "Okay, got to get back. So, don't worry about him not answering your calls, we've got it on our end."

"Love ya!" we shouted, and Stella disconnected.

Just before six, all of our phones dinged with a text message from Carter. Of course, he had figured out the culprits, not that it was difficult, I was sure.

CARTER: Taking my new woman out for dinner to celebrate my birthday.

ATTACHED WAS a photo of the sheep, but at some point

during the day, someone had dressed her up, and she wore a mop head wig and tons of makeup.

A second picture followed of the poor sheep deflated with the pin from the badge sticking in her.

CARTER: Sorry. I didn't know she was a virgin when I popped her.

WE LAUGHED.

ME: Now EWE have to marry her.

CARTER: Haha, very clever. But who the hell wrote this? You still have your caller ID blocked.

SCROLLING THROUGH SETTINGS, I found the switch and turned my number back to show.

ME: It's me.

CARTER: Please tell me that this was your idea.

ME: Why?

CARTER: So, I can think of ways to punish you.

. . .

EVERLY: Really, how?

PIPER: TMI

ARIEL: Y'all do realize that your texts are going to all of us, right?

STELLA: Yo, bro, I have a gift for you. Should I leave it at Sophie's?

VIVIAN: Would you be specific please?

LEO: Yuck, stop.

CARTER: All of you might as well unblock your numbers, I can figure out who is who by your texts. Everly, Piper, Ariel, Sis, Vivian, and Leo.

STELLA, Ariel, and Leo promptly switched their phones to show caller ID.

EVERLY: Bite me.

. . .

PIPER: Still gross.

ARIEL: Perv.

SIS: Can I leave the gift or what? Can we focus here?

VIVIAN: ☺

LEO: Still TMI

STELLA RAN OUTSIDE and was gone for a few minutes before she strolled back in with a large gift bag and a devious smile.

"What did you get him?" I rolled my eyes, not trusting Stella at all.

"None of ya damn business. Now stay out. Ariel, you still have that tape?"

Ariel walked over and grabbed the tape from her purse and handed it to Stella, who proceeded to tape the top of the bag shut.

"Shit. I have got to go," Ariel said. "Kayson will be home soon, and we're going out on a date tonight."

"Got to get going as well. Need to be at the hospital. I work midnight to eight and want to catch a nap first." Stella gave me hug. "Tell my brother that I said, 'Happy Birthday.'"

"Will do."

"I'm going as well." Leo stood and moved toward the door. "Have fun tonight." She winked before heading out, "I'll see you tomorrow, right?"

"Yep. I'll be there."

I waved goodbye to them and then looked down at my phone. Carter would be here in thirty minutes. Running upstairs, I changed into a long flowing sundress and decided to go sans sandals. I put on some fresh makeup, smiling at my reflection in the mirror for the first time in a long time. Carter made me feel beautiful.

I had just gotten back in the kitchen and turned down the heat on the oven when the heavy clanking sound from the garage door opening was followed by the rumble of Carter's Harley pulling in.

When he walked in, it was as if I had never seen him before. His blond hair was messy, and he was in his uniform. He radiated power, and I was powerless to resist him. I had the strangest urge to dip him in honey and lick him all over. A weird memory from when I was a kid hit me. I'd get together with my cousins and we'd fight over who got more *kououmpiédes,* they were our favorite cookies. I would lick them and then set them to the side, my mom would tell me, "If you lick it; it's yours." A devious thought crossed my mind about trying that with Carter. If I licked him did that make him mine?

Chapter Sixteen

CARTER

*S*he was standing in front of the stove, something so mundane and still she took my breath away. The only words I had to express at this moment were, oh shit.

She was just staring at me. "Happy Birthday, ewwwee look nice."

"Very funny. Remind me never to piss you off. If you can think of this and get deputies and dispatch involved for my birthday, I'd hate to see what that mind of yours can conjure up when you're mad."

"Well, your sister helped."

"I think that the two of you are not a good combination."

"Really? That's what Ariel and Leo said. But I think we have so much in common." Sophie batted her eyelashes, feigning innocence.

I walked over to her. "What smells so good?"

"So, does that mean you like Greek food?"

"I love eating Greek." I waited for the moment until she caught my double entendre then a soft pink tinted her cheeks. "The food is good, too."

"Good, that's about all I know how to cook."

"Let me go change, I'll be right back. Do you need any help first?"

"No. Go change."

After getting out of my bulky uniform and securing my sidearm, I headed back to the kitchen and struggled not to go over to her and ram myself deep inside her. She was leaning down, and her perfectly round ass was sticking up in the air and pointing toward me. I let out a soft groan. I was dying to sink inside her. Fuck dinner, I wanted to go straight to dessert.

"Did you hear me?"

I jerked at her words.

"What?"

"I asked if you'd grab us some drinks. What were you thinking about?"

Sinking to my knees, I lifted her dress and looked up. "I was just thinking how much I wanted to be with you or on you or in you, but right now I'd settle for a quick taste of you."

I craved her. I smiled when my hands slid the rest of the way up her legs and I was met with nothing but silky-smooth skin. She wasn't wearing any panties. I cradled her ass cheeks in my hands and pulled her close so I could nuzzle her pussy and give a quick swipe with my tongue, just a tease to get our night started.

"You're only going to lick?" Her pout was adorable, but I licked her again, and a whimper escaped her mouth. I smiled, happy fucking birthday to me.

Forcing myself away from her, I distracted myself with getting us drinks and setting them on the table, which Sophie had set with candles and fine china. "Both of these from my sister?" I pointed at two gifts.

"The bag is, the box is from me."

"Soph, you didn't have to get me anything. Dinner is plenty."

"Oh stop. Let's eat, and then you can open gifts."

Sophie carefully placed chops and potatoes on each plate with green beans and carried them to the table. Holding out her chair, I scooted her in before taking my seat.

It only took one bite of the lamb chop for me to be in love with her cooking. "You're a great cook."

"As if I had any other choice. I'm Greek; they throw us in the kitchen as soon as we can stand."

"Besides inflating a giant sheep and getting it into the station, what else did you do today?"

"Believe it or not, the sheep ordeal took a big chunk of the day. Oh, and I went to the grocery store. I didn't do a cake."

"I have another idea for dessert." My cock was rock hard just thinking about it.

"I made dessert, just not a cake." Sophie stood and went to the kitchen, returning with bowls of powdered sugar, cinnamon, and squeeze tubes of honey, chocolate, and caramel syrups.

Picking up the chocolate sauce, I eyed it mischievously. "Now we're talking, this is exactly what I was thinking of for dessert."

"Oh, you were thinking that you wanted *loukoumades* as well?"

"Louka what?"

"They're small fried donuts. I figured that you could dip them in whatever you wanted."

"No, I was thinking of drizzling that syrup somewhere else and licking it up."

"My plan was that . . ." She shifted in her seat, clearly liking the idea as much as I had. "While we eat dessert, you can open your gifts." She slid a box over to me. "Something about this made me think of you."

Removing the cream ribbon with the brown Bloomingdales logo, I unwrapped the box and slid out another box. Amourage. I had no clue what that was. Lifting the lid, I realized it was cologne with a bottle of after shave and shower soap.

"I can't explain it, but when I smelled this, a memory of you leaning over my car filled my head. It just reminded me so much of you. I liked it."

Lifting the lid, I sprayed a small amount into the cap and inhaled. It smelled like something I would wear. But it was from Sophie, so it just became my favorite cologne. Reaching for her hand, I tugged her and pulled her out of her chair and over to me. Lightly squeezing her hips, I separated my legs and pulled her in so I could rest my cheek against her flat stomach.

When she wrapped her arms around me and leaned over, resting her head on top of mine, I knew that I had to have her for the rest of my life. "Thank you." Then I turned her and pulled her down onto my lap, asking, "Do you remember your birthday?"

"Yes." She smiled and held her arm out to show me the charm bracelet. Sliding it around her wrist, I stopped when I saw the familiar crest shape of the charm I'd had made for her.

"You still have it."

"Yep, never took it off. It's been soldered back on a few times, but yeah, still have it. I think it was my way of keeping a part of you when I knew that I had to let you go."

"Life is full of would have, should have, and could have, but I wish that you would have . . ." I stopped that line of talk when she started to laugh. "What's so funny?"

"Nothing. Go on."

"No. Not until you tell me." Shoving my hand under her skirt, I squeezed her knee, and she let out a squeal. "Ticklish? I'll just have to tickle it out of you."

"Okay, okay, okay. But you can't tell a soul."

"Cross my heart."

"When you said 'would've, could've, should've', it reminded me of the other night when all of you got those text messages. It was the name of the game we were playing. I was the one who came up with letting everyone text whomever they wanted from someone else's phone. Vivian got my phone, by the way."

"We'd figured out you all must have switched phones. If Vivian texted me, who did you text?"

"I grabbed Leo's phone so I texted Ian. It wigged me out a little bit that I was texting my cousin, but I got over it. After all, it was for the greater good and all that."

"What do you mean?" I hadn't seen Ian's messages, but if they were anything like mine. . . I was sure they were interesting.

"Leo has had a crush on Ian since we were little. He doesn't know it. But I think that the two of them would be great. They're both so smart, they like mechanical things, and they both have this brooding side to them."

"First, don't get into the matchmaking business, please. Invite Ian more often and give him and Leo a chance, but don't force it. And second, I think on girls' night out, we just need to assume all fucked-up shit that happens in Central Florida is a culmination of the seven of you."

Her laugh set me on fire and every nerve in me was pulsing, my cock was dying to come out, and I still had to open my sister's gift and help Soph clean the kitchen before I could get her upstairs. "Have any clue what's in the bag?" I was wary, it was from my sister after all.

"No." Sophie pulled in her bottom lip, obviously having the same apprehension.

Carefully pulling the edges apart to rip the tape, I opened it and removed the wadded up tissue paper and froze. Holy. Shit. Stella.

"Where exactly did you get that sheep from?" I raised a brow in question.

Sophie's face turned red.

"Were you with Stella when you bought it?"

"No. No. No. She had a basket full of stuff that she was buying. Ariel, Leo, and she were filling it. No." Sophie stood and ripped the bag from my hands and peered in. "I'm going to kill her. Them. I'm going to kill them. Carter, I'm so embarrassed."

Letting out a chortle at the sight of Sophie's embarrassment, I couldn't contain my smile. "Don't be, it's funny. They pulled one over on you. Welcome to my world." Dumping the contents of the bag onto the table, I looked at the items the girls had thought important to give me. "Edible body dust, hmm. Warming lubricant, I wonder if that's for your pleasure or mine?" Sophie smacked my hand. "Cock rocks, not sure I like the sound of this, let me read, hold on." She made a grab for them, and I shooed her hand away. "Ooh, yeah. We're definitely taking these upstairs. Silk rope? Handcuffs? We could do some role playing with these things." I finished tossing all the stuff back in the bag as Sophie blushed scarlet.

"Sit. Let me put the food away and then we can do . . . whatever." Sophie stacked the plates and took them to the kitchen.

"I can help."

"No. It's your birthday."

"I want to get to the 'whatever' part faster." Together we had the table cleared, the food wrapped and stored, and the dishes loaded in about ten minutes.

"Want some wine?" Sophie grabbed a bottle from the fridge and set it on the counter before reaching to grab two glasses.

"Sure, where's your corkscrew?"

"Right there." She pointed to a black tube plugged into a socket. "Electric. I like my wine."

"Hmm, nice to know. Now, what were you saying about getting to whatever?"

Chapter Seventeen

SOPHIE

I was practically bouncing off the walls. I was confident that my editor was going to love my idea for the new series, and I was going to spend the day with my bestie, Leo. More than that, though, was that Carter had a great birthday, and because of that, I couldn't have wiped the smile from my face if I tried. I quickly dressed in Harley gear and ran downstairs to my office. Gathering my notebook, some extra pens, and a list of notes that I had made to ask Leo, I shoved it all into a book bag before turning off the lights and heading for the kitchen to eat a quick bowl of cereal. Halfway through, I grabbed my phone and shot Carter a quick text.

ME: Leaving in a few, will be with Leo.

CARTER: Have fun. See you tonight.

. . .

HE REALLY WAS TOO good to be true, and tonight couldn't come fast enough. After grabbing my bag, I headed out to meet Leo at the Harley dealership for my first interview with her.

"Mornin', sugar," a man said as he held the door for me.

"Good morning. Thank you."

Leo was waiting for me, and I was taken aback by her appearance. If I hadn't known her almost my whole life, I wouldn't have recognized her in her grease-covered jeans, button-down mechanic's shirt, and bandana wrapped around her head. She looked rather masculine if I were being honest.

"Is this what you always wear?"

She nodded and gave me a weak smile. "I know, this is why I hated that you texted your cousin. He wears ties and shit to work. I'm sure he has more than twenty suits in his closet." She held out her hand to show me the grease smudged across her knuckles.

"I think you're beautiful. And Ian may be a rocket scientist, but don't forget that he also actually builds things. He likes the mechanics and how things operate. Just saying . . ."

"Okay, enough about me. Let me give you a tour." Leo had always hated being the center of attention, so I didn't push.

I followed her around a giant bay of stations where several mechanics were working on bikes. She was explaining the schooling required to be a motorcycle mechanic and then the specialty training for each manufacturer when she was paged over the intercom to come to the front counter. Following her, I spotted a smoking hot deputy—*my* smoking hot deputy —leaning against the counter and I moved straight for him. I could only see his profile. He wore dark sunglasses, his ass filled his pants perfectly, and his muscular tanned arms held a phone up against his ear.

When I was near enough, he snaked an arm around me

and pulled me close as he ended his call and slipped his phone into his pocket. "Hey, princess, I didn't think you were here yet. I didn't see your car."

"It's in back where Leo told me to park."

"Oh." He leaned down a placed a kiss on my lips.

God, he was so fucking hot in his uniform that I wanted to jump him. A tingle rippled up my legs and rested right at my core. I had to fight the urge not to pull him out to my car and head home.

"Sorry to interrupt your lovefest, but whatcha need, Carter?"

"Hey, sorry, Leo. Bike has stalled out on me three times this morning."

"Let me take a look, hopefully you just need a new battery. Ready, Soph?"

"Sorry, gotta go." I smiled at Carter as he tugged my hand and pulled me in for another quick kiss before releasing me. I caught up with Leo as she was opening one of the overhead doors.

"All law enforcement is priority when they are on shift, we get them in and out as quickly as possible. So, Carter jumps to the front of the line. Let me grab his bike, and you can follow behind me." Leo started his engine and drove it in to her station. "I'm going to run diagnostics on it first. All newer bikes have a computer system, which will usually tell us what's going wrong." Leo pressed a few buttons and then typed into a computer. She connected a cable to his bike and let it sit for a second before clicking a few more keys.

"What's wrong with his bike?"

"It's in his fuel lines. Let's go tell him. Probably got bad fuel somewhere."

I listened as Leo and Carter talked bike stuff and I made a few notes on ideas for my story.

"It's going to be a little bit, but I'll hurry," Leo said to Carter before she headed back to his bike.

"You having fun?" Carter placed his index finger under my chin and lifted my gaze to his.

"Yeah. It's neat. A little too dirty for me but kind of cool. She's really smart."

"You're just as smart and"—he picked up my left hand and turned it over, showing me ink smeared across my wrist —"your job can be messy."

Giving him a shrug, I headed back to Leo, who had the bike on a platform raised so she could work on it without bending over or the bike falling over. I was writing what she told me when Carter's voice broke through my mechanic lesson. He tried to mask the tinge of panic that was slowly bubbling up, but I could see his lower jaw quiver.

"Leo, how long?"

"Umm, forty-five more minutes, you okay?"

"Carter, what's wrong?" I reached for his hand, and he pulled me next to him.

"Can you do me a favor?"

"Sure, anything," I promised.

"Will you take me up to ORMC? I just got a phone call. They wouldn't tell me anything over the phone. Just to get up there."

Visions of Stella filled my mind, and it must have done the same to Leo's because she was already pulling her phone out.

"Yeah. Let's go." I started for the entrance and stopped when Leo shouted.

"It isn't Stella. She has no clue why they called. She got off an hour ago, but she'll head back up. She's about thirty minutes away."

I gave Leo a wave and raced with Carter to my car. We were only ten minutes from Orlando Regional Medical

Center, but hopefully, I could make it in less. We didn't talk the entire way. I had no clue what was going through Carter's mind. All I could think of was his mom or dad, but he had said they didn't live here. I parked and then turned to him.

"Want me to come in?"

He nodded, and then we were both striding to the front doors. When Carter gave his name, the woman at the sign-in desk immediately picked up her phone and called someone. Stepping aside, Carter waited for whoever had been notified.

The doors opened and the clacking of heels on the travertine floor echoed around me. When I looked up, a middle-aged woman in a gray suit was coming in our direction. She wore a hospital ID clipped to her jacket pocket.

"Hi, Mr. Lang?" At Carter's nod, the woman continued. "I'm Betsy Cameron, would you like to take a seat?"

"No. I don't want to take a seat. Just tell me why you called me. I'm losing my fucking mind here."

"I understand"—She looked directly at me—"If we can have a moment of privacy please."

"It's fine. Sophie can stay."

I let out a sigh of relief. I didn't want to leave him, but I would have if that was what he wanted. He was losing it, and this crazy woman was dragging whatever it was out. God, this was torture.

"Very well. Mr. Lang, I'm sorry to tell you this, but earlier today, your wife was in a fatal car accident. Your children are fine. The baby . . ."

I swatted the thousands of bees that seemed to be swarming around me at that very moment. Wife? Children? Baby? What? Carter was married? He had a family?

My stomach lurched, and everything around me seemed to be caving in. For a moment, all I heard was the doctor's voice all over again. What were they saying? Cancer? I had cancer? But I was only eighteen, breast cancer, me?

Suppressing the urge to throw my hands over my ears to try to silent the crazy chaotic sounds that seemed to be echoing from everywhere, I took a step back. I wasn't eighteen. I was twenty-eight, and I was standing next to Carter . . . who was *married*. With *children*.

I'd been sleeping with a fucking married man with children. His wife was pregnant. He told me that he didn't have kids. He fucking lied to me. I took another step back, then another, and before I realized it, the swishing of automatic doors opened, and I was out of the hospital.

"Sophie, wait."

Tears streamed down my face as I took a deep breath and turned to face him. All the anger at life's injustices bubbled up, ready to spill over on to this man at this precise moment. Bending over to rest my hands on my knees, I tried to get my lungs to work right. "Wait?" I panted. "You want me to fucking wait? For what? Your children to go off to college . . ."

"No—"

"Shut up, just shut up. You motherfucking liar. You lied, Carter Lang, you lied. You don't get to talk, not now, not ever. You're right, my leaving was wrong, but I had a reason—a life-or-death reason. But you? What was your fucking reason? Your dick forced you to do it?"

"Soph, if you'd—"

I shook my head, fury and anger and soul-crushing sadness warring for the top spot inside me.

"No, damn it. No, I won't listen. You need to go back in to that hospital. You need to go in and be a *dad*. You need to forget my name, my number, forget that I ever existed because, believe me, I'm sure as hell going to be forgetting that I ever knew you."

He took a step toward me, reaching for me, and my last hold on sanity broke. "Don't you touch me. Don't you dare touch me. I wasted ten years dreaming about you. You were what I imagined every hero in every book to be like, but you were the villain. I hate you. I'll hate you until the day I die." I turned around and darted for my MINI.

Cutting through cars, I pulled out my key fob and pressed unlock as I neared. Opening the door, I jumped inside, locked the doors, dropped my head to the steering wheel, and let the gates of my emotions rip open. Rocking my forehead back and forth, the pebbled grip from the steering wheel slowly penetrated my sense of emotions and broke through to my brain just enough to tell me that I was rubbing my head raw.

Slowly, I started my engine and pulled out of the parking spot to head home. I replayed the events of today and couldn't get that woman's words out of my head; his wife, your children, the baby. No wonder he didn't care that I couldn't have children. He already had some. For all I knew, his kids had been at the community center that day and I had seen them. Did he have boys, girls, or maybe one of each.

After pulling into the garage and closing the door behind me, I sat and looked at myself in my rearview mirror. I had a nice firm indent in the center of my forehead from my textured steering wheel, raccoon eyes, and a snotty runny nose. I'm positive that I looked like someone who needed rescuing. But no one would want to touch me for fear of being contaminated. Almost like when parents decided to just cut the fucking onesie off the baby because it's covered in crap and the thing isn't worth salvaging, or the way they hold the baby out in front of them as they try to hose the kid off and not vomit at the same time. That was me. I was too gross to handle or get near, I was easily discarded.

Getting out of the car, my body ached as if I had just been hit by a Mack truck. I tossed my phone and book bag on the table, and managed to make it to my room before collapsing.

Some people eat when they're stressed and depressed, but I sleep. The moment I touched my bed, my body shut down, and I went into hibernation.

Chapter Eighteen

CARTER

"What's going on?" I turned at the sound of my sister's panicked voice as she ran to me, looking around. "Who's hurt? No one will tell me anything."

"Stel, hold on a second." Turning to the receptionist, I asked, "Is there a room that we can go to?"

"Sure, follow me."

We followed her into a side office where I had Stella take a seat and I knelt in front of her. "Listen, this is a long story, and it happened six years ago. Do you remember that trip I took to Vegas?"

"Yeah, but what does this have to do with you? Why were you called to the damn hospital for an emergency?"

"Stella just shut up, will you? Let me explain. When I was in Vegas, well, I sort of got married."

"What do you mean sort of? Either you're married or you aren't."

"When I was there, I met a woman named Ivey, and she and I spent two weeks in a drunken stupor. One night, we got the idea to repeat the *Hangover* movie, including walking into and interrupting someone's wedding. That led us to the next part as you can imagine, making the wrong decision, and getting married. We were so drunk. I was leaving the next morning, how we found our way back to the hotel is beyond me. I didn't even remember anything until I got the actual license in the mail. I knew that I needed to contact her, but the truth is, I never pursued it. It was on my list of things to do, but . . ." I locked eyes with my sister, who had finally relaxed her look of horror and anger. "I just never thought that it mattered until Sophie came back. It doesn't matter, though. Ivey was killed in a car accident this morning. That's why I was called here."

"So, let me get this straight. You married some chick in Vegas, never got divorced, and she died?" Her mouth opened and closed, and I waited. It didn't take long until her eyes narrowed, and she cut daggers my way. "Does Sophie know?"

"She was with me when we got here." I left off that she also heard everything the nurse told me and probably wasn't ever going to talk to me again. Still, Stella saw it clear on my face.

"You freaking idiot!" She exploded. "I can't believe you, Carter. You didn't tell Sophie, the woman you are madly in love with, that you are . . . were married, and this is how she finds out?"

"When Sophie came back, I contacted a lawyer and started the paperwork to get the divorce. I never planned to keep it from her."

"And you think that's enough? I can't believe you, Carter. How could you not tell her? Did you think saying that, oh gee, I forgot I am married would work if she ever found out? Were you just dicking around with her emotions? Because if you truly cared about her, then you would have trusted her and not kept secrets."

"Stella, stop, please not now. I love Sophie, and I will fix this, but right now, I need to find out what happened."

The door opened and Ms. Cameron, the hospital administrator entered. "Mr. Lang, I'm sorry for your loss. Stella." Ms. Cameron nodded her acknowledgement, clearly already knowing my sister. "Mr. Lang, we need you to come downstairs and identify her body please. When you're done, come back here, and I will have all the paperwork together for you."

As pissed as my sister was at me, having her hand in mine was comforting as we were escorted downstairs to the morgue. When they slid the white-sheet-clad body out, I took a deep breath. My heart ached, not because I loved her but because this was someone that I knew. We had spent almost two weeks together; laughing and enjoying nights of wild sex. It had been nothing more, but she was still a human being with hopes and dreams and aspirations. Oh, my God, she was a Mom. "Yes, that's Ivey." I confirmed after they lowered the sheet.

He slid her body away, and Stella and I headed back upstairs and into the tiny room. I needed to unravel what was going on, why the hospital listed me as Ivey's next of kin.

"Mr. Lang, again I am sorry for your loss." Ms. Cameron slid two notarized documents over to me. "The girls have been checked out and except for a few scrapes, they are fine. You will need to hand both of those forms to the security attendant at the play center before they will release the girls to you."

My sister looked at the papers, "Gir—"

"Stella, let Ms. Cameron finish, and then we can ask any questions." I pressed my foot on top of hers as a signal for her to shut the hell up.

"They are in our observation area at the children's hospital. Do you have questions for me?"

"What about the baby?" I tried to act as if I knew what I was talking about since she had mentioned a baby earlier.

"We were able to save the baby, she's in NICU. I will let one of the doctors fill you in on her prognosis."

"When can I see her?"

"Any time. These are your wife's personal items that were retrieved from the accident." Ms. Cameron picked up a large black bag and passed it across the table. "Take all the time you need. When you're ready, Stella can show you up to the neonatal unit as well as over to the play center."

"Thank you." I held on to the bag in front of me and waited for Ms. Cameron to leave before opening it.

"What was that all about? Children? Plural. And a baby?"

"I have no clue. I'm hoping the answers are in here." I upended the bag, spilling a few random pieces of little girl clothes, some papers, and a blue purse onto the table. I reached for the purse and pulled out the wallet that was inside. Scanning her license and the information inside, I was stunned.

Picking up my phone, I called Kayson.

"Hey, how are you? Are you still at ORMC?"

"You know?"

"A little, Leo has texted Ariel, Stella has texted Ariel, and in return my phone has been buzzing like crazy. What can I do to help?"

"I need you to run a license and tell me who is listed as her contact in case of an emergency." After rattling off Ivey's license number, I waited for DAVID, our computer system, to return the information.

"You are, and you're also listed as her spouse. Carter, you care to tell me why this Ivey woman has you listed as her husband?"

"Kays—"

"Are you married? Does Sophie know? Oh God, Sophie? Carter is she with you?"

"Kayson, stop. This has been a giant misunderstanding."

"So, you're not married?" Kayson's anger seeped through the phone.

"Yes. I mean no. I mean it was a drunken mistake six years ago that was never righted."

"Mistake? You're married and it was never righted? Where the fuck is Sophie?"

"She left." God, that hurt so fucking bad to say. "I'm guessing she went home." I waited a second for the moment of tense silence to ease. "Kayson, I love her, and you have to trust me when I say that I will explain everything. It isn't what it seems. Please just call Sophie. She left before I could explain and I need to know that she's okay. I need her to listen to me."

"I'll call Sophie. What can I do for you as your sergeant?"

"Can you schedule me off for this week?"

"Will do, take some time. Let me know if you need anything else."

I disconnected, Kayson's words hitting me, *what can I do as your sergeant?* He didn't ask *what can I do as your friend?* I'd hurt his cousin and to him family came first. I went back to Ivey's purse trying to erase those thoughts and concentrate on what was in front of me. I froze when I pulled out her insurance card. There were three names listed: Ivey Lang, Harlow Grace Lang, Gianna Marie Lang. According to the card, Harlow was five, and I added nine months to the date listed and she absolutely could be my daughter almost to the day. Gianna, however, absolutely could not be. She was two, and I knew this new baby wasn't mine, either.

Stella jingled a set of keys. "I'm assuming one of these goes to whatever address is listed on her license." Stella continued rummaging through the items on the table while I looked at the information and receipts stuffed in her wallet. I was struck with pangs of guilt for puzzling together a woman's life, a woman who was technically my wife, possibly the mother of my child, and she was a stranger, a drunken mistake that I never corrected because I had given my heart away years before and was never taking that chance again.

"I don't think there is anything else here. Let's go up to the NICU and check on the baby before we go get the girls. We can then go by her house and try to figure everything out. You're going to need car seats." Stella pushed her chair out and stood.

I was always the strong one, but right then, it was my sister, and I was glad that she was there. In our careers, we both saw a lot of death and unfair shit, but it was different when it was happening to us.

Riding the elevator up to the NICU, I rested my head against the cold steel, exhaustion hitting me as if I'd been running a marathon. When the doors opened, I followed my sister and listened while she stopped to speak to a nurse that she knew. We were led to an area with giant glass windows. I peered at babies who were in their own little glass boxes covered in tubes. Some were so tiny I didn't see how they'd survive.

"She went to get the doctor. But Ivey's daughter is right there." Stella pointed to the fourth box that held a small precious girl covered in tubes. "You were listed as the father. Carter..."

My sister's fingers wove in between mine as she gripped my hand tight. "You might be a dad to one; you might not be a dad at all. What are you thinking?" Her words were gentle while still prodding.

I took several deep breaths and tried to clear my head. I met my sister's eyes. "I think there are three little girls that have just lost their mom and are in need of a protector."

"What about their dad or dads?"

"You and I both know, if they were anywhere around then Ivey wouldn't have named me. She did this for a reason."

"What reason?"

"I'm a protector. It's my job." My heart picked up speed at my words. I knew there was something very right with what I had said.

"The nurses asked that when you come to a definite decision as to what you are going to do, too, please let them know."

I was confused, not sure exactly what she was asking.

"What I am trying to say is, you have three options. You can wait to see how the baby does health wise. Or if you know that you want to find a loving family, one of the nurses will call a counselor. But, if you are positive that you are her protector they'd like a name to call her."

Staring at the tiny girl, who had her whole future in front of her, I whispered, "Avril Stella."

Tristan stepped up behind us. Just the sight of Sophie's cousin had a ton of bricks settling in my stomach.

"Come with me." His words were soft but clipped.

We followed him into his office where he shut the door.

"I'm really confused, especially since you've been practically living with Sophie, but right now, I'm going to speak to you as a doctor only. The mother was still alive when the paramedics arrived on scene. They asked her if there was anyone she wanted them to contact. She begged them to call you, and she named you as the baby's father. When she arrived at the hospital, she crashed. We did an emergency cesarean, and we listed your name for the hospital paperwork and forms for the birth certificate."

"Her name is Avril Stella." In a day filled with uncertainties that was the only solid that I knew for certain, the only thing I felt as if I had control over.

"We'll have that added to the birth records," Tristan said as he continued. "You, of course, can always do a paternity test and have your name removed or elect to forfeit all rights. As far as the baby is concerned. . ."

"Avril Stella."

"I'm sorry what?"

"Her name is Avril Stella. Stop calling her 'the baby' as if she is an it."

"Fine. I'm sorry Carter. You know that I meant nothing by it. Avril Stella is at thirty-four weeks, which is good considering the circumstances. We're going to have to keep her while her kidneys finish developing, but a baby born at thirty-four weeks seldom has any lifelong health concerns or developmental issues."

Shoving my hands through my hair, I tried to grasp everything, but it was a lot. Almost too much.

"Avril's going to be fine and grow up to be gorgeous and healthy and happy."

Tristan's words finally sank in. She was going to make it.

"For twenty-four hours, we will keep her environment contained. You can see her, but you can't hold her. We want to ensure that her system has stabilized since she has gone through a traumatic shock."

I nodded. "But when I can see her?"

"Now. You can see her now, you can even stay here with her if you want. She is listed as Baby Girl Lang, but of course we will have that changed to Avril immediately." Tristan stood and shook our hands. "How are you holding up?" he asked Stella. I saw her give him a slight smile.

"Let's go see her and then I can take you to get the girls?" Stella grabbed my hand and pulled me to the viewing area.

Avril's tiny fists moved, and she let out a small yawn.

What am I going to do? Leaning my forehead against the cold glass of the giant window, I pleaded for an answer, any answer, just something to tell me what I was supposed to do. I wanted to run away and go find Sophie, but I knew I couldn't. I was the last person she wanted to see. Hell, according to her, she hated me and never wanted to see me again.

I would fix this.

I had to.

There was no way I'd lose her again.

My eyes found the tiny baby in the incubator again, and my heart sank. I wasn't sure that I could raise three girls. Where was their father . . . or fathers? I could very well have a daughter I had no idea existed, and a tiny part of me hated the idea that Ivey kept that from me. I wasn't even given the opportunity to discover whether or not I'd be a good father. If Harlow was mine, I'd missed her first steps and first words.

"Come on, let's go meet the other girls. Do you think that you'll know when you see her if she's yours? Like, this super possessive parental super power comes over and says, 'she's the fruit of my loins'?"

"You're the fruit, and I have no fucking idea." Her strange mental thought process managed to pull a half-smile out of me.

Stella led us to a walkway that connected ORMC to the Arnold Palmer Hospital for Children. Following her through a maze of hallways, we came to a large reception desk in front of a giant play area where I handed over the paperwork to the woman behind the counter and then turned to stare. One of those girls could be my daughter, and I'd missed five years. Trying to get a glimpse of a face, eyes, something that would tell me that I had been a dad and never knew it, I took a seat and waited.

The receptionist picked up the phone on her desk and called someone. A woman inside the play area moved to a phone on the wall and answered it, I followed her eyes as she scanned the room, where were her eyes focused? When she hung up, she typed into a computer then walked over to where two little girls were sitting and having a pretend tea party. The older one stood and grabbed the youngest by the hand then they followed the woman to the doors.

When the doors opened, we stared at each other. The blonde little girl was the spitting image of Stella. The two girls were escorted over to me, the youngest burying her face into her big sister's side.

"Hello, Harlow. Hi, Gianna," I said as I sat on the floor at their level.

"You're a policeman?" Harlow asked.

"Yes. I'm a sheriff. It's like a policeman." I had totally forgotten that I was still in my uniform.

"Our daddy is a policeman."

My breath hitched at those words. Did Ivey tell Harlow about me or was there someone else?

"Where is your daddy?" My sister got down to their level and reached her hand out to pet Gianna's head.

"I don't know. Never met him."

"Can I tell you a secret?" I reached for Harlow's tiny hands and looked into her face. If my sister didn't see what I was seeing, she was crazy. I knew without a doubt that she was my daughter. I didn't need a paternity test to tell me. Harlow's blue eyes, which mirrored mine and my sister's eyes, were enough for me. "I'm your daddy."

The air around me was charged from Stella's heavy stare, Gianna lifting her head, and Harlow's quivering lip. I held my arms out, and both girls threw themselves in and I wrapped them tight.

Could I do this? Looking down at these two little girls that had just lost their mother and had nowhere else to go, I knew I had to try. With Sophie's help, I knew that I could do anything. But, what if Sophie didn't want to or wasn't willing to help? Could I still do this?

Thousands of questions were painted across Stella's face, and I knew that she was fighting to hold her tongue.

Pulling back, I stood with Gianna in my arms. Holding Harlow's hand in mine we headed back to the elevators and downstairs to the ground floor where we stopped and purchased a car seat and a booster seat.

For the first time, I was grateful that Stella had driven her car. It only took me a few minutes to secure them, but getting the girls settled took far longer.

"Where's your Jeep?" Stella asked as we all settled into her car.

"I've been staying with Sophie, it's over there."

"Hold on, will you?" I motioned to her with one finger and jumped out, closing the car door behind me so that the girls couldn't hear.

Dialing Sophie's number, I cringed when it went to voice mail, hung up, and sent a text instead.

ME: Please call me ASAP. It isn't what you think. Ivey and I got drunk six years ago while I was on vacation and got married. It never went beyond my vacation. Please let me explain. I need you. Please.

BUT NO FLASHING bubbles appeared to tell that she was writing back.

Dialing Kayson, I figured that he would be able to give me the best advice.

"How are you?" he asked as way of greeting.

"Not good. Ivey had three daughters, and for some reason, I have no fucking clue why, she listed me as the father."

"Whoa. What?"

"That is all I know right now. We're going to go over to

Ivey's apartment and see what we can find out. Stella's probably calling Ariel right now and asking her for help as well."

"Well, speaking of Ariel, she went over to Sophie's."

"And . . ."

"And what? Nothing, she isn't answering her door and won't pick up her phone. She's blocked us out again, and right now, to be honest, I'm holding you responsible."

"But she won't listen to me. I just need her to listen so that I can explain."

"Did you not have a single chance over the past month?" Kayson's reply cut deep. "I've talked to her mom and have tried to fill her in on what little I know. But she seems to believe that Sophie just needs time to process everything and has asked for us to give her space."

"Space? For how long? Another ten years? I can't." A burning in my chest was the only thing that reminded me that I hadn't just died at the thought of another ten years without her.

"I don't know what to tell you, man. Sophie's mom assured me she will reach out when she's ready."

"I'm in love with her."

"Until Sophie is ready to talk, leave her be. If you push this and she runs again, you will have more than just me to deal with."

The sound of my phone clattering to the cement followed by the smooth swish of it sliding across the pavement echoed around me. I held on to the side of the car to stay upright as my whole body shook. The last thing Sophie said to me was that she never wanted to see me again, and I didn't think any amount of time would change her answer. *Please, Soph, just give me a chance to explain.*

Chapter Nineteen

SOPHIE

I was curled up under the covers and hugging the pillow that Carter had slept on for the last few days as banging wiggled its way into my fog-drenched mind. Thankfully, I was able to tune it out and go back to sleep.

Ringing crashed through my nightmares and forced me awake. Stretching my hand out to silent the god-awful noise, I knocked something over. Shit. The ringing continued. Lifting my head up, I realized it was my phone, my house phone. Fuck. Only one person had that number.

"Hello?" My voice creaked.

"Sophie, honey, were you sleeping?"

"Yes, Momma, I'm really tired."

"Okay, precious, call me in the morning, please eat. I know you, Sophie, you can sleep for days."

"*S'agapo mom.*"

"*Agapi mou.*"

I hung up and nestled back under the covers, my mom's words falling flat against the hollowness in my chest that roared louder reminding me that I'd lost everything all over again. I drifted back to sleep remembering the words the lady at the hospital said, "your wife, your children, the baby."

Chapter Twenty

CARTER

*S*tella drove while I stared at the cracked screen on my phone.

"Sophie?" She reached over and placed her hand on mine for the briefest second.

"Yeah. I've been trying to call her all day, but it just goes to voice mail."

"Give her some time. She'll call back."

I didn't believe her, so I kept silent. "Kayson said that she isn't answering for anyone, and that I'm to leave her be until she's ready to talk. How am I supposed to leave her alone, Stella, tell me? I just got her back."

"I don't know. But we'll figure something out, okay?"

"She's done, she won't give me a chance to explain."

"How would you feel if you were in her shoes? She feels as if every time something good happens in her life it is doused ten times over by something bad. I'm not trying to be mean but the first man a girl ever loves is her daddy and Sophie's died when she was little. Then she fell in love with you and was forced to leave."

"Do you know why she left?" I asked, not really knowing

how much Sophie had shared with the girls if any.

"No."

"She had breast cancer."

"Oh God, I'm so sorry. I'm so sorry for Sophie, she's so young, fu . . .fudge, we are all so young. But, ten years ago. . ."

I had kept my eyes on the girls in the backseat. Holding my hand out to Harlow and she held tight. Gianna had fallen asleep almost instantly, lulled by the hypnotic sound of tires on pavement. But Harlow was just now giving in, her eyes drooping, her grip loosened, and her hand fell to her side.

"And all this time, she's been tied up in knots, still pining away for you. Now she returns only to open her heart, fall in love, and discover that you're married with a child." Stella flipped the turn signal and then cut right into my complex. "I wasn't exactly feeling sorry for you before, but now I'm really having a hard time. I know that you're stressed, you have a lot on your plate, and you have some big decisions to make but you haven't lost hope." She pulled into my reserved spot and turned off the engine. "I think that you should stay with Harlow and Gianna. What if I get Leo, Ariel, and anyone else that can go with me and we head over to the address listed and gather some things and bring them to your place?"

"You don't mind? It's getting late." I let out a yawn as the exhaustion and worry from today took its toll on me.

"Of course not. Do you have a garage opener to Sophie's so we can get your Jeep? Leo only has her bike and not much will fit in here."

"Crap."

"What now?" Stella let out a long sigh.

"The garage opener is on my bike at Harley."

"We'll figure it out." Stella opened her door and got out.

Peeling myself out of the front seat, I was moving slower than normal, every muscle in me ached. I turned around and pulled my seat forward to reach for Harlow while Stella unbuckled Gianna, both of whom were sound asleep.

"Hope is the only thing that keeps us going in this world. Sophie doesn't think she has any hope left. You were her second chance, and she probably thinks she just lost you again. You need to figure out how to reach her."

Balancing Harlow in my arms, I fumbled for my keys and then fumbled some more to open the door. There had to be a trick to juggling a sleeping kid and opening doors. Moms did it all the time without dropping anything. I managed, but just barely, and we tucked the girls into my bed before backing out of the room slowly.

Stella and I were just sitting down in the living room when there was a light knock at my door. Opening it, I saw Leo, Vivian, Ariel, and Kayson standing there. "Come on in, just keep it down."

"Can we start from the beginning?" Leo asked, her eyes bouncing between Stella and me.

I was too tired, so I let Stella handle it. I even kept quiet during her disparaging remarks when she told them about Ivey and me and how I neglected to tell Sophie about the marriage."

"What happens now?" Leo looked as if she was going to be sick. I understood that feeling, she loved Sophie and she knew that Sophie had to be hurting.

"What about the baby? Who's listed as the parents for the birth certificate?"

"Her name is Avril, and yes, Ivey told the hospital that he was the father, so they put his name on the paperwork. From the insurance card that we found, I'm assuming that she must have done the same for Gianna, but I want to see what we can find out. When you see the girls, you'll understand my confusion."

"Why is that?" Leo asked.

"I'd bet a million bucks on Harlow being my niece. She looks just like Carter, well like me." Stella dropped her head to rest in her hands.

"But the other two, where are their dads?" Ariel asked as tears rolled down her cheeks.

"Not sure, which is where all of you come in. While Carter stays with the girls tomorrow, I want to go over to the address listed on Ivey's license and see what's there. Let's see what we can use and pack it up, and then we can search to see if we find anything that will give us any clues. We'll also need to get clothes, furniture, and all the kid stuff."

"What if the place is bigger or has a yard, why not have Carter just move there?" Vivian offered.

"Ummm, it's on Americana Boulevard."

Everyone let out an, "Oooooh."

Hell, Orlando PD only had two murders and a handful of drug busts in the last week there, so truthfully it was getting better.

"I'm off, why don't I see if one of my brothers can go with us. The girls can pack up while we keep watch, and then we can load up and get the hell out."

"Daddy?" We all turned at the sound of a tiny voice. Harlow was standing in my bedroom doorway peering out. The women let out low gasps as soon as they saw Harlow, whose resemblance to Stella was uncanny.

I held out my arm and waved for her. "You can come out here." She ran to me and buried her head in my lap. Tilting her head, she peeked out and smiled at each person. Her eyes illuminated with excitement.

She only knew of her father from stories but tonight it all became a reality. Her little mind must be doing somersaults. I wasn't a small man and could be intimidating, and with Kayson and all these women, none of whom she knew but all of whom were staring at her with looks of wide-eyed shock, she was probably overwhelmed. Harlow surprised me when she smiled as if they were all here to play with her and headed straight for the group. She was definitely related to my sister.

"Daddy, I need to go potty." Harlow crossed her legs.

Shit. I hadn't even thought about that.

"Come on, sweetie, it's in here." What was I supposed to do? I opened the bathroom door, and Harlow raced in, pulled off her pants, and sat on the toilet. She didn't even care that I was standing there. Was it okay that I was standing there? Oh, shit, how did these things work? I looked up at the sound of Kayson chuckling, only to see the women all smiling back at me. "What? I'm not sure that I'm even allowed to stand here and watch while a five-year-old goes to the bathroom." They all laughed some more.

"It's fine, you are definitely her father, you'd win that million-dollar bet. Stella has a mini me," Vivian said, and I let out a long sigh.

"I know, right? She obviously got her good looks from me." Stella beamed.

I turned back at the sound of a grunt. Harlow was stretching, trying to reach the faucet. "Step stool. I need to get a step stool." Moving into the bathroom, I picked her up so she could reach the sink while she washed her hands.

"On it, I'll start a list." Ariel pulled out a notepad and pen.

Holding Harlow's hand, we walked back to my living room. "Would you like to meet these people?" She nodded, so I introduced her to everyone.

"My sister Gia is sleeping in Daddy's bed." She announced and then happily went to Stella, obviously recognizing her from earlier. She sat in Stella's lap while Stella finger combed her hair and we continued to make plans for tomorrow.

Stella looked over to Leo. "Can you go by the shop and grab the garage remote from his patrol bike before we meet in the morning?"

"Sure, I can get in at seven."

"Awesome. Thanks. That gives us Carter's Jeep, Kayson's truck, and Everly's Suburban to use to haul stuff tomorrow. Wait . . . does Everly work tomorrow?"

"I'll text her now." Leo pulled out her phone.

I kept my head buried in my hands, trying to absorb this change in my world when I felt my sister's hand on mine. "You know I'm always here for you, right?"

"Yeah. Don't get all mushy on me, kind of scares me, it makes you unpredictable, it's out of the norm."

"Oh, fuc—unny, I'm going to have to learn to watch my language."

Stella trying not to say fuck was going to be very funny.

"Everly is calling in tomorrow, she'll be with us."

"Great. Let's meet at Ariel's"—Ariel nodded her okay —"tomorrow by eight, I know it's early, but if we get there before neighbors in that area actually wake up, we can avoid any drama."

"Smart plan," Kayson and I both said in unison.

"Now, for the pink elephant in the room." I slid down in my chair at my sister's statement, and rested my head against the back. "Who is going to be responsible for getting the truth to her? She needs to know." Leave it to Stella to get right to the point. "If I have to stand outside with a megaphone and shout it, so be it, but I figure one of you might want to be more diplomatic." She pointed to everyone else.

"Let's think about it." Kayson's firm voice invited no arguments. He leaned over and saw that Harlow had fallen back asleep in Stella's arms.

Stella was rubbing her hand up and down Harlow's back and caught Kayson's stare. Figuring that he wanted to talk about the girls, she stood and carried a sleeping Harlow back to my bedroom.

"Let's finish talking about everything else. The girls, what do they know? Do you know anything about Ivey's parents or any other family?"

"No. Nothing. We haven't spoken since Vegas."

"What are you going to tell the girls? They are going to start asking where their mom is." I looked at Kayson, surprised. How the hell did he know this shit?

"When Sophie's dad died, she had a million and one questions. She and her mom stayed with us, and even though I was only, like, seven at the time, I still remember it. She and I would talk about when he was coming home. My parents tried to explain it, but it was Damon who actually got through to us."

"How?" I was exhausted but needed to know how to handle the next few days.

"I always carried this Batman action figure around. Damon took it from me and stuffed it in his shirt. He asked if we could see Batman, and we both said no. He asked us if we knew Batman was still there, and we both said yes. And that was exactly how it was with Uncle Nick, Sophie's dad. We wouldn't be able to see him anymore, but we would always know that he was there."

"Gotta love kids," Stella whispered. I stared at my sister. Under all her false bravado, she was a sucker for those that couldn't take care of themselves. It was why she was an awesome nurse.

"Can I say that I just fell in love with Damon?" Vivian laughed. "Those are powerful words even for me to take in and know that my husband is still here."

"Okay, enough mushy shit." We all snapped our heads to Stella. "Sorry, crap. Let's call it a night and meet at Ariel's in the morning. Carter, have you checked Gianna to see if she's wearing a diaper or Pull-Ups?"

My eyes must have gotten as big as saucers because I had

no clue what a Pull-Up was and the thought of diapers totally grossed me out.

"Get used to it, Avril's gonna wear them for a few years." Stella gave me a wicked smile. "You all go on home. I'm going to stay here for a bit before heading out. See you in the morning."

I walked everyone to the door and gave each of the girls a kiss on their cheeks. Kayson leaned in and patted my back. "I talked to my aunt, one of us will get through to Sophie. Let's not have the girls do it. When she learns the truth, I want them to all be friends again. Family she has to forgive."

I nodded, knowing that he was right. I didn't want my mistake to put a wedge between her and the girls. "Please do it quick. I love her, Kayson."

"Wow, I never thought that I would hear you say those words. I'll do whatever I can."

I locked the door behind him and went to find Stella, who walked into the kitchen at the same time I did.

"She wears Pull-Ups. I'll run up to the 7-11 and grab a small pack for the night."

"Thank you. I really appreciate it."

"Any time, Carter. I'll be right back." She placed a hand on my shoulder and peered into my eyes, searching for some answer. "You think of anything you need, call me."

She must have decided against whatever she was going to say and right now, I was grateful. My mind had slowed to a crawl.

"Okay."

"I'll be right back."

She left, and I headed to the bathroom to change. It was a whole new world of wearing clothes to bed. Fuck, I needed to get a better gun cabinet. Damn it, they hadn't eaten, they were going to be starved when they woke up. Leaning over the counter, I slid my hands down my cheeks and stared at my reflection in the mirror. Was this fair to the girls? Was I what was in their best interest? Was this what Ivey wanted, was this why she named me as their father?

Was it because she knew I would protect them if something ever happened to her? Remembering the story Sophie had told me about how her cousins had reacted to her crush on the lifeguard, I thought about what kind of father I'd be—I'd probably be worse. I'd probably chaperone them or follow them until they were thirty.

Kids were raised in single-parent homes all the time and some were single fathers, right? I could do this. It was Avril who I was most worried about. Do they have preschools for newborns? If not, could I afford to have someone here the days that I worked? Splashing some more cold water onto my face, I snapped myself out of this daze and walked out of the bathroom just as the sound of a key jangled in my door.

Stella entered with several bags.

"I thought that you were just getting those pull things."

"Pull-Ups. Yes, I got those, but I also got some other stuff. They're going to want breakfast, and we might be longer than lunch, so I got a box of mac 'n' cheese. Plus, I got these." Stella held up two dolls with tiny bodies and gigantic heads and far too much makeup. "They're stupid, I know, but it was all the convenience store had."

"Just in case I forget to tell you, I love you. You're a great sister."

She bumped my shoulder. "Go get some sleep. I'm going to head home. Oh, might I suggest sleeping in your own room, but curl up on the far side of the bed. The last thing you want is for them to wake up and be scared to death in a strange room, especially Gianna. Little kids have the lungs of a banshee. Go. They will probably be up in a few hours anyway."

I followed Stella to my door, and then I watched her get

into her car before turning around and locking up for the night. Turning off the lights, I picked up my phone and dialed Sophie as I padded back to my bedroom. The call went straight to voice mail, I disconnected, then crawled into bed, and lay on the far side. I patted my pillow and after that remembered nothing else.

Chapter Twenty-One

SOPHIE

T he roar of a Harley was getting closer and closer and closer until finally it rumbled one last time and cut to silence. I threw back the covers and ran across the hall to the balcony that overlooked the front yard. Leo was in my driveway, and Stella was getting off the back of Leo's bike. They both stared up at my house, I moved back to the corner and peeked around the curtains. Letting out a small smile, I saw Stella on her knees, hands together praying, as if she were begging me to let her in, but I wasn't ready.

What was it Carter had said, no excuses because they only pleased the person that was telling them?

The mechanical grinding of gears echoed as my garage door lifted, and a few seconds later, Carter's Jeep appeared and the clanking of the door lowering sounded. Leo drove off, waving back at my house as Stella followed close behind in Carter's vehicle.

Heading back into my room, I picked up my house phone and dialed my mom.

"Hello, precious child."

"Good morning, Momma."

"What's on your calendar for today?"

"Nothing, I just want to sleep."

"Sophie, that isn't good. Call Kayson please. If no one else, call Kayson or Leo."

"I'm not ready to talk to anyone."

"Sophie, you need to listen to them, things aren't always what they seem. Kayson and I had a long talk."

"Mom, please. I can't."

"Fine. Don't forget to eat something."

"Okay, Momma, *S'agapo*."

"*Agapi mou*."

I hung up, turned my head and pulled Carter's pillow to my face, I inhaled deeply. His strong woodsy masculine scent had made me feel protected. Now it reminded me that I was alone and would always be alone. God, I loved him so much, this hurt so bad. Why did he have to lie? I never lied to him. I tried to handle things on my own but I had never lied, not once. I expected cancer to hurt, death to hurt, but not love, love wasn't supposed to hurt worse than all of those combined.

Pulling the covers over my head, I fell back asleep, this time it wasn't a peaceful sleep at all.

Chapter Twenty-Two

CARTER

"*H*umph." I was startled awake as a little girl landed on my chest. Clearing my sleep-dazed mind, I saw four bright eyes peering at me. "Good morning."

"Morning, Daddy." Wrapping an arm around Harlow, I pulled her in close for a hug. Gianna was still not talking and standoffish.

"Morning, Gianna. You need to go potty?" She shook her head.

"You hungry?" She nodded.

"Can I have a hug?" She shook her head.

"Okay, let's get up." Rolling out of bed, I held out my arms, and Harlow jumped into them so I could swing her around before setting her on her feet. I held out my arms for Gianna, but she crawled to the opposite end of the bed and dangled herself off until I helped her down. Okay, Gianna and I needed to bond.

"Harlow, you go to the potty first and then we'll take Gianna." Gianna met me with a stare that would have made Stella proud. She may not be mine, but she had my sister's personality down to a science. "Harlow, when you're done can you help your sister?"

"Yes, Daddy, she needs little girl underwear."

Shit, fuck, what were little girl underwear? I nodded, backing out of the room slowly until they couldn't see me, then I pivoted and ran to the kitchen so I could upturn the bags of stuff Stella bought last night. I thought Stella said that Gianna wore those pull things. Grabbing the pack that said Pull-Ups, I brought them to the bathroom and opened it, holding one out for Harlow. "These?"

"Yep. Gia is supposed to wear little girl underwear until she doesn't have any more accidents. Then she wears big girl underwear like me."

Ahh, got it. Little girl and big girl. "Do you want to put on one of my T-shirts so you're in clean clothes? It will be like a long dress?"

Gianna's eyes lit up for the first time. Finally, I had hit on an idea. Racing back to my bedroom, I grabbed two OCSO T-shirts and went back to the bathroom. Harlow and Gianna were standing there in only their underwear, big girl and little girl, and they were adorable. "Hands up." They both held their hands above their heads, and I slipped the first one over Harlow. It rested right at her ankles. I slipped the second on Gianna, and it engulfed her.

Think, Carter . . .think.

"Hold on, be right back." I ran into the kitchen and grabbed a roll of duct tape out of my junk drawer and pulled off one long piece as I ran back to the girls. I split it down the middle to make two long, narrow pieces before rolling Gianna's sleeves and looping the strips through each armhole. It was like those buttons and loops on some of my button-down shirts.

The shirt itself was still too wide and too long, so I pulled off several more pieces of tape, bunched the back of the shirt, and secured the fabric in place. From the front, the shirt looked tailored. Deciding that I'd just have to cut the length, I scooped her up and headed out to the kitchen where I grabbed the scissors and had her twirl while I cut around the bottom so that the shirt rested just above her ankles. "You look gorgeous." She gave me a smile. I kissed her nose. "Let's wash those hands, and we can eat."

Picking up the girls, one under each arm, I held them over the kitchen sink. Harlow turned on the water, and I waited as they washed their hands giggling. Turning back to the counter, I saw what Stella had bought for breakfast. "You want Frosted Flakes or Froot Loops?"

"Froot Looooops!" they both shouted.

The girls took seats at the table while I tried to figure out how much cereal I was supposed to give them. Crap, how much did kids eat? Were they like dogs? Was I supposed to measure the food? Was it so many cups per pound or by age? I read the back of the box, but there were no fucking instructions about feeding. So, deciding that more was better than not enough, I filled their bowls to the rim before dumping in milk.

Big mistake! I quickly learned that they didn't eat a lot, and that the more I put in the bowl the more there was to splash on the table, the floor, and on them. By the time they were finished with their breakfast, which was only about four minutes, I hadn't even poured my own bowl. I decided that I would be a parent who supported television time. Sitting the girls on the couch, I picked up the remote control and started flipping through the channels. Shit. I made a mental note to call Direct TV and get a block put on the adult channels. As I was scrolling through, trying to find something that said Kids Network in the title, they let out a yell.

"What?" I looked around the sofa to see if something was wrong.

"Go back, Daddy, go back."

Scanning back through the channels, their faces lit up when I passed the Disney Channel so I left it there and saved it as a favorite channel on the remote.

While Gianna watched, Harlow carried on a conversation.

"Mommy has 'nother baby. It's a girl, too. Do you know where mommy is? They wouldn't let me or Gia see her. Gia cried, I hugged her and told her not to cry."

"That was very brave of you not to cry and to help your sister. You're a good big sister." Harlow smiled at the praise. I remembered the dolls that Stella had purchased. "I have a surprise for you." Gianna's head whipped in my direction, her attention immediately focused on me, and I smiled. Another win. "Hold on."

"Daddy," Harlow said as she giggled.

My heart did this weird skip at the sound of being called daddy, I hadn't known until that moment that I wanted kids. But I did.

I ran to the kitchen and snagged the dolls from the bag, tucking them behind my back as I walked back to the girls. "Close your eyes." When both of their faces were squinted tight, I dangled the dolls in front of their eyes. "Okay, open."

Shouts and squeals rang out, and I made a mental note to get more dolls.

My phone dinged at that moment and I got up and walked back over to the kitchen counter to pick it up.

STELLA: Just got to apartment. Place is a dump but looks like Ivey tried to keep inside her apartment clean. I hate to keep asking, but are you 100% sure?

· · ·

I BENT over the counter and rested my head on my forearms, wondering for the millionth time in under twenty-four hours if I was doing the right thing.

A touch, light as a feather, grazed my leg, and I looked down to see Gianna in her duct-taped, cut-up T-shirt, holding out her arms toward me. Scooping her up, I snagged my phone and headed for the couch, getting comfy with Gianna on my lap and Harlow curled up next to me while we watched some show about a girl with super long hair, a horse, and a chameleon. Opening my phone, I texted Stella back.

ME: 100% sure.

STELLA: Gathered what was worth keeping. Got all the girls' stuff, and she had already gotten some baby stuff, but most of it was really used so we are leaving it. Returning key to office. Kayson is going in to try to get the security deposit back. We put everything outside the apartment, and within seconds, it was gone. No one asked if we were stacking it there to take downstairs, it was just gone, all of it. Ariel has a list of stuff the girls need. Damon is going to check and see what they have in a few of their model homes.

ME: Thank you. Tell them thank you.

STELLA: Should be on our way in about twenty minutes.

ME: Okay. Watching some show on Disney Channel.

• • •

STELLA: LOL

I WENT BACK to my main text screen and checked the ones that I had sent Sophie yesterday, but they were all still unread.

Just under an hour later, the sound of laughter filtered through my door. Harlow stood on the couch and Gianna scooted closer against me.

"It's okay, it's just Aunt Stella."

My small two-bedroom condo suddenly felt even smaller with six women, plus Kayson, Ian, and Tristan.

"Wow." Tristan walked over to Harlow and held out his hands. He was a natural with children, I guess that was what made him a great neonatal doctor. "Yeah, no need for any blood tests. If I didn't know the story, I'd assume she was Stella's. Wow."

"So, where are we unloading everything?" Kayson asked, stopping next to the couch with a box in his arms.

"In my spare room. I figured that we could make that the girls' room."

All eyes turned to me, I knew what they were asking, the same thing that I'd been asking of myself: could I do this?

"Look at her, she looks just like Stella, there is no denying it."

"I know, I know. But what about Gianna?" Gianna lifted her head and looked at Kayson. Ariel smacked his arm, and I'd never wanted to deck him more than I did then. "I'm sorry. I didn't mean for it to sound like that, really. We'll talk later."

"There's no need. I won't separate them. I've made up my mind. Regardless of what you all think." I wanted to lash out and demand that they leave the girls and me alone and tell them that we would figure this out without all of the judgments, but I bit my tongue.

"Well, then, girls, you can direct and organize?" Ariel, Leo, and the others nodded before following Kayson's orders.

"You and I need to have a seat at the table, I have some stuff for you to see," Stella said as she held up a manila envelope.

"I'm going right over here." I pointed to the table as I slid Gianna off my lap and stood. "You girls just watch cartoons, okay?" They nodded, but Gianna turned herself so that she could see the television and still see me, which made me smile.

Once I was sure the girls would be okay, I took the envelope from my sister and opened it. Inside was a copy of Harlow's birth certificate, which had my name listed as the father. I pulled out the second birth certificate, which also had my name listed as the father. I looked up and gave Stella a questioning look.

"There's no way."

"I know that, and you know that, but the only thing that matters is that piece of paper. Unless someone challenges you to a paternity test or you want to have a paternity test done to prove you aren't their dad, you are, by all rights, the legal father."

Reaching back into the envelope, I pulled out the last two items, a copy of our marriage license and Ivey's birth certificate.

Piper was walking in with a box at that moment. "Can you call this in to the station and see if either of her parents are still alive." I handed her the birth certificate before turning back to Stella. "That's all there was?"

"We found some bank info and old bills and there's a baby book for each of the girls. As much as I don't like this, I have to say it looked like she tried to be a good mom." Stella grabbed my hand. "The girls shared a room, and from what I could see, Ivey slept on the sofa. Carter, I know you are doing this, but are you financially ready?"

"Yeah. I'll do whatever I can. There's a lot of single parents making it on less than I make and I've been saving most of my checks for ten years."

"Okay, let's do this." Stella stood and walked into the girls' room.

I loved my sister more than ever at that moment. She didn't say good luck, instead she had included herself in helping to raise the girls. I looked over to where Harlow and Gianna were jumping on the cushions as they watched each familiar item from their old home be brought into my condo, their new home. It was only a matter of time before I was going to have to explain.

"That's all of it," Kayson said as he clapped his hands. "By the way, what is she wearing?" He pointed at Gianna. "Ariel come here, did you see this?" Ariel came running, followed by everyone else, and they all started laughing at my alteration handiwork.

"Leave me alone, it was the best I could do."

"Sure." Kayson smacked me on the back. "Ariel, why don't you and Stella take the girls into the room and have them help you all decorate."

Ariel picked up Gianna while Stella grabbed Harlow and they headed off to the spare room.

"We're going to take Ariel's list and get a few things you need." Leo waved the notebook in the air as she and Everly headed out the door.

"Let me get you my credit card."

"We got it, we can get some of this." Vivian gave me a hug. "I'm proud of you. I think that you are doing the right thing." She and Piper raced out the door to catch up with the others.

"At least someone does."

Kayson, Tristan, and Ian moved into my living room and took a seat, they all wore looks to kill.

"What's up." I dove right in, ready to break the ice.

Kayson rested his elbows on his knees. "We need to talk about Sophie. We understand the whole story, we know that you're in love with her, but what if she doesn't give you the chance to explain?"

"She has to."

"No, she doesn't," Ian corrected me. "Don't you get it, we still have no clue why she left ten years ago."

I opened my mouth, stunned.

"You know?" Ian leaned in. "Tell us, we need to know."

"I can't. If you want to know, you're going to have to ask her yourself. Don't you get it? I've already broken her trust. I'm in enough hot water with her. I'm not sinking in any deeper."

Tristan opened his phone and scrolled until he found whoever it was he was looking for and called. "Yes, it's all done. Listen, I don't care what you have to do, get Aunt Dion to force Sophie to a family dinner. It is time some stuff is discussed." He waited while whoever—I assumed his mother or father—spoke on the other end. "No, don't care. She comes to dinner tonight or the four of us boys are breaking down her damn door." Ahh, he's talking to his dad. "Pops, Carter knows why she left ten years ago and he won't tell us." He paused for a moment, his eyes finding mine as he smirked. "Yeah, I know. We're family, but she doesn't trust us. Well, it's time she had a wake-up call, the world doesn't stop moving and we don't disappear just because she does. She needs to remember that she has a lot of people who love her. Family dinner or broken door, don't care." Tristan disconnected.

"I always thought you were the mellow one." I looked at him in a whole new light.

"He is the mellow one. We wouldn't have given the option of a family dinner." Ian waved between himself and Kayson.

Chapter Twenty-Three

SOPHIE

y house phone rang and then stopped. I laid my head back on the pillow, and it started ringing again. This time, I leaned up to answer it, but it stopped again. I moved my hand back and it started ringing again. I snatched it from the cradle ready to rip the head off whoever was on the other end.

"What?"

"It's Mom."

I let out a sigh; her voice was abrupt. A forewarning that this wasn't her normal coddle me phone call.

"Family dinner tonight at six at your Uncle's house."

"Too tired, don't feel like coming."

"You don't have a choice. Tristan said you either show or he is going to let his brothers use their idea for getting into your house. Soph, don't play around. You know them. That is Tristan's way of warning you that you are out of chances."

"I know. But, Mom, I just . . . I'm not ready."

"Sweetheart, I suggest you get ready, like, now. For ten years, they've been driving me crazy and I kept quiet because you asked me to. But you and I both know that doesn't work in Greek families, we're back. They are tired of the secrets. They love you unconditionally, you need to give them the same love in return. If you wanted the ability to keep secrets, you were born in the wrong family. You have four hours."

I dropped my phone onto the mattress without disconnecting and got out of bed. I was in zombie mode, having been out of commission for hours, which meant it was going to take me four hours just to wake up. I stumbled downstairs to fix myself a bowl of cereal—the first thing I'd eaten since yesterday morning.

I spied my cellphone on my table, the same spot where I had left it yesterday. Pressing the on button, I waited for it to power up while the emptiness of my house hit me. Except for the crunching of my cereal, the sounds of *ding, whoosh, ding, ding, whoosh* overtook the room as message after text message came in and voice mails piled in for the party.

"Siri, play my voice mails."

"You have twenty-seven voice mails. Please delete to make room for incoming messages. Here is your first message from Carter, dated Tuesday at eleven . . ."

"Sophie, where are you? Please, I need you."

Siri ran through call after call from Stella, Leo, Ariel, Kayson, and my mom. Every one asking me to call them back, but it was the last message that made me stop chewing and listen with undivided attention.

"Here's your message from Carter on Wednesday at one AM . . ."

"Soph, please I need you. It isn't what you think. I wanted to tell you. I was *going* to tell you. Six years ago, I had just made motors and had two weeks before my official start day. I headed off to Vegas and took my first vacation. I stayed drunk the entire time, and I made myself a promise that when I came back I was going to stop obsessing over you. It was sort of my give-up-on-Sophie drinking binge. I met Ivey, one night we drank too much, and at some point, we got married. When my vacation was over, I headed home. Soph, I didn't care about getting a divorce because I wasn't ever getting married. I knew that I'd never give my heart away. I'd already given it to a brown-eyed girl who I had met ten years ago when I had pulled her over for speeding and I never forgot her. After you got back, I contacted a lawyer to have him draw up the papers. Don't you get it, Sophie? It's you. It's always been you." There was a pause, but I could hear his labored breathing coming through the speaker before he continued. "As far as the kids . . . Ivey had three. Harlow is the right age, so she could be mine. All I can say is that there had to be a hole, a rip . . . something in the condom. The other two definitely aren't mine but I don't care, you should see them, they are beautiful. And when Harlow calls me 'daddy', it just does something to me. Please, Soph, please. Don't cut me out again. I know that three kids are a lot, but I'm keeping them, I'm going to raise them. They've lost everything, they need me. Okay, that's all I wanted to say. I love you, Soph. I love you with everything in me."

I listened to Carter's breathing and waited for Siri to tell me it was the end of the voice mail, but the sound of feet moving played back through the speaker. I laughed at the sound of what I had thought was running water at first to only realize it was him peeing, then the flush of the toilet, followed by him washing his hands. He must have thought he had disconnected. I listened as the phone hit something—if I had to guess, it was him setting his phone on his nightstand. A second later, there was the clear sound of covers shifting and then . . .

"Siri, replay last ten seconds of voice mail."

"Replaying last ten seconds of voice mail from Carter on Wednesday at one AM . . ."

Turning my volume up, I leaned in and waited.

"Goodnight, Daddy."

Whoa. That was what I thought I had heard. Carter had what I had always wanted him to have, what he deserved. He had children. My left arm went numb, my chest ached, and I couldn't catch my breath. In my mind, I knew that I truly wasn't having a heart attack but more like a heart-breaking-attack.

Leaving my bowl on the table, I dashed upstairs, turned on the shower, and jumped in.

"Holy fuck, that's cold!" I screeched, dodging the spray for a minute before washing my hair, shaving my legs and armpits, and jumping out. I quickly dried off before throwing on some light makeup, and grabbing a sundress from my closet. Back downstairs, I picked up my phone and sent a text.

Me: Talk?

Stella: Abso-fucking-lutely.

Me: In person. Where?

Stella: ORMC?

Me: See you in twenty.

I grabbed my purse and headed into the garage, which had this bizarre empty feel. I had gotten so used to having Carter's Jeep and motorcycle there that it was unsettling to find them missing. I envisioned bicycles and tricycles stacked in the corner. Wiping away the tears, I put my car in reverse and headed up to the hospital.

Me: Here. Where are you?

Stella: Do you know where Tristan's office is?

Me: Yep.

Stella: Head toward there, I'll meet you by nurse's station.

Me: On my way.

Stella waved at me as soon as I stepped off the elevator, but before I reached her, a nurse stopped me with a smile.

"May I help you?"

"I'm Dr. Christakos's cousin, and I'm here with Stella." I pointed over toward where Stella stood.

"Let me give you a name tag, and you'll be free to go."

I wrote my name in the visitor's log, grabbed the sticker she held out for me, and walked over to give Stella a hug. She was standing in front of a window, eyes fixed on one of the tiny bassinets.

"Do you see the little girl over by the wall?"

I looked, trying not to get too transfixed by the beautiful little babies in the room, and then nodded when I spotted the little pink hat.

"That is Avril Stella Lang."

Those pains returned, numbness, ache in my chest, only this time not a shortness of breath. Instead it was my very last drop of oxygen escaping in a whimper.

"What's wrong, Soph?"

"Back when Carter and I first met, I told him that I was going to name my first child Avril."

"Ahhh, so that's how he came up with the name so fast. I thought maybe the man had been secretly playing on Nameberry."

"What about the other kids, are they okay?"

"They're fine. Can you believe it? Carter is going to have three daughters. That's what I call karma." Stella let out a laugh.

"Is it terribly wrong of me to want to hold her? I understand if you prefer I don't without Carter's permission." I looked around the area, suddenly sick to my stomach. "Wait, where's Carter?"

"He came up earlier." Stella pointed to a side room next to the nursery. "It's fine. I just need to give permission, Carter listed me on the security forms." Stella walked over and spoke to a woman and then returned. "Okay, you'll have to go in there and put a gown on over your clothes then slip booties on over your shoes. There's a rack with packets of iodine soap filled scrub brushes by the sink. Be sure to scrub your hands really well."

Doing as I was asked, I peered through the glass and kept my eyes on Avril as I scrubbed my hands and under my nails. My heart ached. She and her sisters were going to grow up without a mom. I was so close to my mom that I couldn't imagine not having her in my life. I turned at the sound of a door opening and saw a nurse, who waved for me to follow her. With Stella by my side, I moved into a small sitting area with rocking chairs and waited. When the door opened again, the nurse returned with Avril. A tidal wave of emotions crashed down on me. I held out my hands and took the precious baby, all I had ever wanted was to be a mom, and this baby didn't have one.

"Hello, Avril, aren't you lovely," I crooned. "You are going to be so spoiled. Your aunt Stella is going to spoil you, and your aunt Ariel, and your aunt Leo, and even me. We—we are all going to spoil you. I'm going to read to you and remind you that you can grow up and be anything that you want to be." I rolled her into my chest so I could reach my eyes with one hand and wipe away my tears. Meeting Stella's eyes, I said, "Please tell me, how much of this did you know and keep from me? Just be honest."

"Nothing. I knew none of it. Soph, I never even heard Ivey's name until yesterday. I'm just as shocked as you are. You know I would have forced him to tell you if I'd known. There's no way I'd let him keep that. Fight club, remember?" Stella gave my knee a light squeeze.

"You know why I left ten years ago?" I didn't wait for her to answer, nor did I look at her. "I found out that I had breast cancer. It was advanced stage three. I'm never going to have kids."

"Soph. . ." Stella's voice cracked as she said my name but I couldn't look at her or I'd lose it. I was barely holding it together just knowing that Carter had gotten everything I had ever dreamed for him, he had a family. But once again, I was the sacrifice. "You know that he doesn't care about any of that, right? I think that he knew you were it for him even back then, he would have gone through it with you."

Wiping another tear away, I powered through. "He's really going to raise all three of these girls as if they are his own?"

"Yep. I believe that Harlow really is his daughter. Somehow, someway, in those two weeks, something happened. Either he has strong swimmers that can break through latex or there was a rip and she was very fertile."

"Probably all of the above." I let out a soft chuckle.

"Probably."

"What does he need for the girls, anything?"

"We still have to go get stuff for her." Stella pointed down at Avril. "She has nothing. No clothes, furniture, nothing. We went by Ivey's apartment, and she had some stuff for the baby but it was so used and handed down that I left it. Tristan said it would still be at least two more weeks before she's released. So, Ariel, Leo, and I are planning to go out this weekend to a few garage sales to see what we can find. You can come with us. Plus, the girls are both going to need new stuff soon, too. What they have will do for now, but it isn't good, and the clothes are all stained. He has a nice savings account, but he will go through that fast, especially if he tries to find a small house where the girls will have a yard to play."

"I can help." I looked down and imagined Avril in a room decorated to befit a Disney princess. "Wouldn't it be beautiful if each of the girls had their own room decorated like their favorite princess? I could just imagine Belle and a room full of books and roses, Cinderella with slippers and mice, and Snow White with trees and apples . . ."

"Yeah. I can picture it. Right now, we just need the basics. You can be the one that goes over the top and buys them the crazy ridiculous stuff, okay?"

"Okay." I peered into Avril's dark blue eyes with amazement. Like many babies her eyes might not remain blue. "Little one, will you have brown eyes, green, or vibrant blue like the man that is your hero? You don't know it yet, but he is a hero, he rescued you and your sisters."

"I'll be right back," Stella said, and I nodded.

As I rocked her back and forth, Avril's eyes drifted shut and her cupid-bow lips dropped open as she drifted to sleep. I must have sat there for twenty minutes before the door behind me opened. When no one came in and the door didn't close again, I pulled my eyes away from her and turned to glance over my shoulder.

When I did, my heart sank. Carter was standing there, holding a little girl in his arms and another by the hand as he watched me.

I smiled at him, but he didn't smile back before turning to someone else in the hall.

"Stella, can you take Avril from Sophie please?"

My heart shattered.

He didn't want me holding his daughter. Standing, I turned and watched Stella push her way all the way through the door. I waited for her, holding Avril tight against me.

"It's okay, baby. I will still buy you stuff, all kinds of crazy stuff and send it via Aunt Stella or Aunt Leo. I promise that you won't ever want for anything. I love you, little one."

At that, I handed Avril over hesitantly. I hated letting her go and tried to mask the tears that were rolling down my cheeks. But it was of no use.

"I'm sorry," Stella whispered.

Leaving the room, I threw the gown into the bin and pulled the door open right before a pair of bright blue eyes captured mine. They were part of a whole package of curly blonde hair and dimples. She waved at me, and I waved back before turning toward the elevator.

"Stop, Sophie." I forced myself to face him. "Follow me." His words were curt.

"Carter, you're obviously busy. We can discuss this later."

"Follow me."

"Daddy."

That single word made my knees buckle, and I grabbed the wall for support.

"Are you mad at me and Gia?"

"No, love, I'm not mad at you or Gianna." Looking up from his daughter, he met my eyes. "Sophie, I mean it. Let's talk." I hesitated for a second as thoughts raced through my mind about whether I could get out of there before he embarrassed me. He was bound to scream at me. Maybe Tristan was here, there was no way Carter would blow a gasket in front of Tristan. "Sophie, don't you dare run again."

His words cut deeply, and I nodded, following Carter to a waiting room where he set the girls in front of a television and turned it to cartoons.

"Shocked to see you here, I figured that I wouldn't see you for another ten years. Imagine my surprise to see you holding my daughter."

"I'm sorry, I shouldn't have held her without your permission."

"And . . ." He glared at me, waiting for something.

"And what?"

He rested his elbows on his knees and stared at the floor. "And you have nothing else to say? How about the fact that you ran away?"

"I needed time to think. It was a lot to take in. It isn't as if I went far. I was at my house."

"You think it was a lot for you to take in?" He huffed. "In the past six months, I've discovered the girl who broke my heart ten years ago, the one that I thought was the one." Carter raised his head, and his eyes blazed in fury. "She wasn't gone, never to been seen or heard from again, in fact she was the cousin of my best friend. Then I find out in the last few weeks that we still had this undeniable connection." He clasped my hands in his, and I felt the heat radiating from him. "Then I discover that she fought breast cancer, went through hell, and back, and never once bothered to tell me or ask if I was willing to stand by her. Then yesterday morning, I find out that"—he lowered his voice—"a woman that I met while on a drunken bender in one of my many attempts to get over the girl who broke my heart had died. And not just that, find out I have a daughter and have missed the first five years of her life. Oh, I don't know, let's top it off with the fact that the woman had two more children and for some reason decided to list me as the father." He stood and peered over me. "You think that you had a lot to take in?"

"But you kept a huge secret. I thought that you were married."

"And had you stayed, you would have learned the truth just like you would have learned the truth if you'd stayed or even called me once you got to California. All it would have taken was one conversation and you would have known that I would have been there for you. Sophie, don't you get it? It's you. It's always been you." He bent his head and shoved his hands through his hair. "I don't want to imagine a life without you. There is just something that happens to me when you're around, everything in the world seems to right itself. This is our second chance."

"That's why I'm here. I realized that I didn't want to blow this second chance."

"And what makes you think that you haven't already blown it?"

His words were a hurricane hitting a tiny flame of hope.

I stood and faced him. "You have a beautiful family."

"Soph, don't. I didn't mean it."

Chapter Twenty-Four

CARTER

*S*ophie turned, and my world fell apart at that moment. All the accidents I had been called to, the people in shock, dying, the strung-out druggies, none of it compared to the void of nothingness I saw on Sophie's face and in her eyes.

I bent and slid one arm behind her knees and one under her arms and swept her up into my arms before bringing her back to the couch.

"Sophie, I'm sorry, so sorry. I was just mad and hurt. I thought that I had lost you again. Please, princess, please. Don't do this, I need you. I just got you back; I can't lose you again." I didn't care who witnessed me baring my heart to this woman or if I looked like some fool with tears running down my face. She was it for me.

Harlow's hand patted Sophie's face. "You're pretty. You look like my Gia."

Picking Harlow's hand up, I kissed it. "Yes, she does look like Gianna." At the sound of her name, Gianna came toddling over and laid her head against Sophie while I cradled her in my arms.

"Daddy, don't cry." At Harlow's words, Sophie cried harder.

"Sophie, please. I need you. We need you. I need your help. We're a family. I want you as part of my family, I have for ten years. Please, I'm so sorry."

"Daddy, why is she crying?" I shook my head because I wasn't really sure.

"Big Gia, why are you crying?" I couldn't help but smile at the name that Harlow had bestowed on Sophie.

Sophie turned her head and stared at Harlow for just a beat before pulling away from me, and I wasn't sure whether that was a good thing or not. She scooted to the far corner of the couch, leaned over, and picked Harlow and Gianna up to cuddle around her.

"I'm crying because my heart hurts."

"Why does your heart hurt?"

She looked over at me. "My heart hurts because I miss things."

"I miss my mommy." Harlow's sad eyes turned to me. "Daddy, where's mommy?"

"Gianna, can I see your doll for a second?" Gianna held it up, and when I nodded, she passed it to me. I knew it was time, and with Sophie being here, maybe she would be able to help since she had been Harlow's age when she lost her dad.

All three of the girls watched as I shoved it into my shirt then glanced over at Sophie, who sat up taller. "Harlow, can you see Gianna's doll?"

"No."

"Is Gianna's doll still here?"

"Yes, Daddy, that's silly. Just because I can't see it doesn't mean it isn't here."

Sophie pulled Gianna closer to her and hugged her.

"That's how mommy is, you can't see her, but she's always

going to be here. She's going to watch you and make sure that you grow up happy."

"But I can still talk to her?"

"Yep, all the time."

"Who's going to take care of me and Gianna?"

"I am. You're going to live with me."

"What about my baby sister? Is she hidden?"

"Nope. Aunt Stella is holding your baby sister in the other room."

"Can we see her?"

"Yep, in a minute." I looked to Sophie, wishing I could reach over and wipe away the tears streaming down her face.

"Harlow." Harlow moved off my lap and over toward Sophie when she said her name. "You are beautiful."

"Gia is beautiful too."

"Yes love. Gia is beautiful too."

Harlow scooted over to Gianna and settled next to her so they could continue watching cartoons.

Sophie smiled brighter and looked up at me. "How did you know?"

"Kayson. I couldn't figure out what to tell them, so he told me about the two of you and Damon. When Harlow asked, it felt like the right thing to say."

"Well, it worked for me, so I'm glad they understood, too."

"I am, too. Would you like to come with us? Gianna and Harlow are going to go meet their sister today."

"It's okay, I'll head home. That's a family thing."

Carter slid his hand across the couch and reached for mine, squeezing lightly. "That's why I want you to come with us."

Sophie stood and I followed. We walked over to where the girls were watching cartoons and picked them up, Sophie cradled Gianna in her arms and I carried Harlow. I wasn't sure if they had realized the truth yet or if it would hit them later. I'd have to check with a counselor about this. We moved to the glass windows to find Stella and Avril.

"About time," Stella said as we came around the corner. "Avril is sound asleep."

"Let's let the girls see her, then we can figure out what to do." I wrapped my free hand around Sophie's waist and escorted what I prayed would be my family to the giant viewing window. "See that baby?" I pointed to the nurse rolling in the cradle. "That's your sister. Her name is Avril." Sophie shivered when I said the name. God, what I wouldn't give to know what she was thinking right then. Did she remember that night?

"Do you see her, Gianna?" Sophie asked, and Gianna nodded. "Oh, crud. What time is it?"

I looked at my watch. "Almost five, why?"

"I have to be at a family dinner at six, no ifs, ands, or buts."

I cringed at the thought, I knew why she had to be there. I didn't want to let her out of my grasp, but I knew that she had to go.

"I have an idea," Stella cut in. "Why don't I take the girls home and get them fed and ready for bed? I can take your Jeep since the car seats are in there. You can take my car, follow Sophie and go to family dinner with her. That way you two can talk afterward." God, I loved my sister. I gave her a smile that said I owe you big time.

"Umm . . ." Sophie pulled in her bottom lip.

"If you don't want to, Soph, I understand, just tell me, but I do think we need to talk."

"No. I agree that we need to talk. I was just worried about the girls. Are you sure they're okay?" She turned from me to Stella. "You can take them to my house, and they can rest on the couch. That way, if anything happens, we—I mean Carter can get there faster."

"Soph, I'm a nurse. All of their stuff is at Carter's. It will be fine."

"Wait, where are they sleeping?"

"They had beds, we set them up in my spare room. Soph, it will be fine. Let Stella take the girls. We need to talk."

Stella reached to take Gianna from Sophie, and for a child that had been so quiet, it was shocking to hear her scream as if she had just had all of her fingers slammed in a door.

"Gianna, shhh. Baby, don't cry. Why are you crying? Shhh, *zoi mou*."

"Gianna, stop, sweetie, Aunt Stella loves you. Harlow will be with you." I looked at Harlow. "Can you get her to stop?"

"Gia, come on, let's go with Stella." Harlow reached for Gianna's hand, and the screams got louder.

"Okay, I'll take them home. I'm sorry, Soph. After dinner, would you consider coming to my place so we could talk, please?"

I let out a sigh of relief when she nodded.

"Okay, Gianna, stop crying. You aren't going with Aunt Stella." Gianna's gut-wrenching sobs slowly ended and were replaced with hiccups. We got into the elevators and headed downstairs. Walking outside, I couldn't help but have a bit of hope at the thought that this could be my family, not just my girls but my sister and Sophie as well.

"I'm on level three," Sophie said as we reached the parking garage.

"So am I."

"I'm over in the next garage in the faculty area," Stella announced, giving each of the girls a kiss goodbye and heading in the opposite direction we were headed.

We headed to the third-floor parking area, "Where's your car?" Sophie pointed straight ahead. "Mine is a few rows over.

So, I'll see you tonight. No matter the time?" I asked, needing to hear her assurance again.

"I promise."

"Soph." Our eyes locked. "I love you."

"I love you, too." Hearing her say those words somehow seemed to right everything that had been going wrong in my world for the last day and a half.

"Okay, Gianna, tell Sophie goodbye. Let's go get some dinner." I set Harlow down and wrapped my hands around Gianna's waist to pull her toward me, which had the blood-curdling cries starting all over again. "What is up, kid?"

"Carter, stop. Her world has turned upside down."

"Gianna, can you look at me?" Sophie tilted her head back. "Would you like to come with me?" Gianna nodded and Sophie glanced to me. "Why not just bring the girls and let's all go to family dinner."

"What about your car?"

"I can follow behind you."

"And leave her screaming the entire ride?"

"Unless you want to put her car seat in my car, then yes."

"I'll put the car seat in your car. Harlow, stay right here with Sophie. Daddy will be right back."

I ran to my Jeep and pulled it up behind her car. If someone had told me a week ago that I would have to mess with car seats, I would have laughed. Yet, there I was, moving a car seat from my car to Sophie's. It was surreal.

"Okay, ready."

I watched as Sophie acted like a seasoned veteran parent and secured Gianna into the car seat, talking to her the entire time. "This is my car. I'm going to be driving so you will be able to see me the whole time, and we can talk and sing songs. Harlow, would you like to ride with me or your daddy?"

Harlow scooted closer to me. She was definitely going to be my girl. I helped Harlow into her booster seat and then got into my Jeep. I started it up and pulled a few spots forward to wait for Sophie to back out of her spot. I knew that she was headed to her Aunt and Uncle's and she had Gianna with her, but for some reason I still wanted to keep an eye on her to ensure that she'd be following me.

Chapter Twenty-Five

SOPHIE

*P*ulling up to my Aunt and Uncle's house, I saw the cars and knew that everyone was waiting. It was three minutes until six. With Gianna in my arms and Harlow between Carter and me, we walked in, and the boisterous voices ceased as all heads turned in our direction.

"Hi."

"Hi?" Aunt Christine asked, walking toward us. "And who do we have here? Hello, Carter, nice to see you."

"Hello, Mrs. Christakos, George." Carter kissed my aunt's cheek and shook my Uncle's hand. "Hello, Mrs. Kostas, I'm Carter Lang, it's nice to finally meet you."

"It's about time, wouldn't you say? And call me Dion, please."

"Very well, Dion. These are my daughters, Harlow and Gianna."

I watched as Harlow said hello to everyone, but Gianna looked around slowly, taking everything in but never once letting go of me.

"*Thée moy mikro*, Sophia."

I looked at my aunt. "Really? You think so?"

Everyone nodded.

"What do they all think?" Carter leaned in and whispered.

"This little girl looks exactly like Sophie when she was small." My mom answered as she headed over to the fireplace and picked up a picture to bring back to us. "See?"

"Holy shit. I mean shoot."

"Can I see, Daddy?"

I swear that my heart melted every time I heard her call him that.

"I told you that she looks like Gia."

Carter let out a laugh. "Yes, you did. They all think you are right." Harlow beamed brightly.

"Well, there is a lot to discuss, and part of it has to do with Carter and these beautiful girls, which is why I brought them. I know you called this family dinner because you want to know why I left and why mom and I stayed away for so long. I brought Carter here because he's part of that reason and he and his daughters are part of my life which make them part of our family as well." I looked over at Carter and saw his eyes close. When he opened them again, he was holding back tears but his smile was huge as he pulled me closer to him. I looked over to my mom. "I love you, Mom. You have been my rock. You're the one that kept me going." I looked at the rest of my family. "Let's all take a seat in the family room."

As we all filed in and found seats, I looked to Carter, who gave me a reassuring smile. He knew what I was about to do and agreed. Carter had explained to me about what had happened six years ago and it was my turn to explain to my family why I left. I began my story with how I met Carter, followed by the doctor's call, the years of battling breast cancer, and then ended with when I came home to discover that Carter and I were still in love with each other. When I was done talking, my cousins were doing their man thing and trying not to cry, my aunt was crying, and my Uncle . . . well, he looked pissed?

"Uncle George, are you okay?"

"No, I'm not okay. How dare you and your mother go over to that land of hippies without family and take on all of that without telling anyone. You two women think that you can handle everything all by yourselves. Well, I'm here to tell you that you might be able to, but why should you have to when you have family willing to help. And why would you cheat us out of being there for you?" He turned on his sister. "I love Sophie like she's my own daughter, and you, Dion, we've always been the closest. Why? Why wouldn't you at least tell us even if you didn't want help? You women, I swear." He looked at Carter. "I pity you, son, you now have four." Uncle George leaned over and placed a kiss on my aunt's lips and then whispered something that made her blush before he left the room. My cousins let out a laugh, and Carter joined them. I looked at my mom, who was shaking her head.

"What did I miss?"

"I have no clue," Carter said.

Ariel was laughing but was the only one willing to explain. "Before you got here, they were all freaking out about what you were going to tell them, but your mom wasn't saying a word. Christine was worried that it was going to be serious and break the family's heart. George promised that he would change the mood if Christine promised to do something, we don't know what that thing is."

My cousins threw their hands over their ears as if they were five.

"Obviously, he is getting whatever it was." Ariel smiled, and my aunt blushed again.

"Let's eat," Aunt Christine said as she stood and walked as fast as she could without running into the kitchen.

We all followed, and I smiled to Uncle George, who

promptly smacked my aunt on the ass as she passed him. Leaning back to Carter, it was comforting knowing that he was behind me. "Have they always been like that?"

"They have. He's worse when it is just the guys around, though."

I held Gianna, and Harlow sat in her own seat as we all ate. My family. I knew it in my heart.

After dinner and a few adjustments to the car seat situation, Carter, the girls, and I were on our way to his condo. The girls had fallen asleep almost as soon as we pulled out of the driveway, but he waited until we were halfway there before he spoke.

"I'm sorry that I didn't tell you. I was trying to take care of it on my own. It didn't even dawn on me to get a divorce until you were back here and we were . . . well, we were we."

"I understand, believe me, I understand better than anyone what it's like to want to take care of things on your own."

"We both just need to pay attention to what your Uncle said. When you have family, why should you have to do anything alone." Carter's thumb rubbed the back of my hand.

"Well, don't you dare tell him he was right."

He laughed. "I won't. Promise."

There was a beat of silence, and then I turned to look at Carter's profile, whispering, "All I ever wanted was you and to be a mom."

"I can give you what you want and what your heart needs." Carter's words had begun to heal something in me that had been broken for years.

I caught his toothpaste model smile in the moonlight, but then it vanished as he turned into the parking garage at his condo.

"You come get Gianna, I'll carry Harlow." Carter reached

in and grabbed Gianna and handed her to me before going around and lifting Harlow.

Together, we got them dressed for bed, and for the first time in a long time, I was full of hope. I had been raised with money, I had a trust fund, I pulled a paycheck from the business my father left behind, and I had my own successful career. But I had always figured that my money would be left to some beloved cousin's child, not my own daughters. I gave the girls each a kiss and Carter and I moved from their room to his.

"Get ready for bed, I'll be right back."

I quickly changed and then curled up on the bed as Carter came in carrying two glasses of water and set one on each of our nightstands.

"Before we say anything, let's wipe our slates. Are there any secrets that you want to get out and haven't? Because I've told you everything, breast cancer, can't have kids, that's it."

"Yes."

Yes? Did he say yes?

I waited for him to continue.

"I'm madly in love with you, Sophie. I hate what happened to Ivey, and I'm doing everything I can to make it right. But, please don't think I'm horrid when I say this." He sat up straighter and clenched my hands in his. "But I'm happy as all fuck to have three little girls, and I'm even happier to raise them with you."

We sat there for what seemed like ten minutes, just staring at each other. "Tomorrow, we are making some changes."

"What's that?" Carter let out a half-contained laugh.

"I'm going shopping, and we are decorating the spare rooms at my house. Decide what you want to keep from your condo or get rid of it. There's that extra room downstairs that could be your office. We can get a better lock on the door, have a safe put in there, and make it a kid-free zone. You know, because of your deputy stuff. Each of the girls will have their own room and I'm not taking any of that stuff." I pointed toward the spare bedroom. "Oh, I need to trade in my Countryman, you think a Land Rover will work for the five of us? I've never driven anything but a MINI, but we're going to have two car seats and a booster seat for a while, so we need the room. Your Jeep won't fit all of us. Do we need two?"

"Sophie?"

"Yes?"

"I love you."

"I love you, too. But I have to think about this. We are probably going to have to divide and conquer and get this shit knocked out. Shit. I mean shoot. I have to work on my language. Wait, Harlow is five. Has she been in school? When's her birthday, kindergarten, preschool?"

"Sophie?"

"I know, I know, you love me. My mind is going a million miles a minute." Carter flipped off the lights, then slid under the covers. It hit me that I was in Carter Lang's bed, I had never been in Carter's bed before. Sure, he'd slept in mine but oh my God, I felt like a teenager again and I was in Carter's bed just as I had dreamed many nights. I slid down, he wrapped his arms around me and snuggled me against him so we were spooning.

Chapter Twenty-Six

SOPHIE

"$\mathcal{T}$he delivery truck is here. Do I even want to ask what you had to do to get them to deliver these items so fast?" Ariel stood in my open doorway.

"No, you don't want to ask. Just have them assemble as much as they can outside before they bring it up. Leo and I are finishing Avril's room now, just need to finish painting the candelabra gold and adding a chip to the teacup."

"We're done with Harlow's!" Piper shouted. "She is going to love what Vivian did, I swear this woman is a fairy godmother. You should see the wall painted to look like a ballroom."

"We need ten more minutes!" Stella hollered. "Everly and I can't get this stupid magic carpet to stay on the wall."

For the last week, Carter and I had lived in his condo. As much as I hated eating my own words, I couldn't get stuff done as fast as I claimed that I could. It took me all day Thursday just to get my car traded in. I would have thought that trading in a paid-off vehicle and purchasing a vehicle with a bank check would be simple, but noooo, they had to try to supersize every fucking thing until I was ready to walk out. Thank God that Carter calmed me down because I was seriously considering telling Gianna that I was going to leave for a bit and let them deal with her screaming until they hurried up.

Friday, we met with the funeral home. Without Ivey having any next of kin, Carter let me help. I convinced him to have Ivey buried even though we weren't doing a service. The girls should have a place where they could go when they got older to talk to their mom.

Saturday, Carter stayed at my house with my cousins and Uncle as they made the house baby proof and worked on his man cave while I spent all day choosing furniture for the three rooms. Sunday was all shopping, too.

Over the weekend, I also discovered that Vivian was an awesome artist, and when she offered to paint murals on the girls' walls, I was indebted for life. This enabled me to bring my princess idea to fruition, but she needed time and help, so we all agreed to chip in. It took us the entire week to pull it all together, but I knew it would be worth it.

"When does Avril come home?" Leo wiped her hands off and started to clean up our area.

"This week. Tristan said that she is healthy and her kidneys looked great. Carter is taking one more week off to help with the transition. Everything seems so surreal. I can't believe it's been a little over two weeks."

"I know, but the girls seem to be adjusting. Do they have any bad moments? How about Carter, does he ever act like this was a big mistake?"

"Yes and no. Yes, to the girls, Harlow will talk to her mom sometimes and then will cry because she can't see her. Gianna just clings to me. I actually spoke to a counselor at the hospital, and she told me that it is her way of grieving and making sure I don't leave as well."

"And Carter?"

"Carter was made for this. It's as if he's been doing this since day one. The man is a pro. I mean, except for the other day when we were online making a list of stuff to get. I thought he was going to have a heart attack."

"Why? Or should I be afraid to ask?"

"Did you know that there are stuffed animals that look like poop? Stinky poo plush toys to teach your child not to be afraid of going to the bathroom. All Carter kept saying was, 'Yeah, just what I want, teach the girls that it's okay to play with their shit. We'll have shit spread on every wall. Hell, let's turn it into finger paint.' Umm . . . needless to say we didn't get that."

Leo and I were laughing as we finished the room and piled all the tools into a box before we headed out of the room to meet with the others downstairs.

"It is going to be beautiful." Stella leaned her head against mine as we all stood outside and watched the men unwrap the furniture. "Are those pieces ready?" He gave her a nod, so she led the way up to Gianna's room.

I had a hard time not following, but that was part of the deal. We had all drawn straws for a room, and no one else was allowed to see any room but theirs until the big reveal. Once Stella was back, Vivian led the men up to Harlow's room, and when they were finished, Leo and I led the delivery guys back up with Avril's gold-leaf crib and matching furniture before rejoining everyone back in the living room. I signed the delivery slips and grabbed my phone to check the time.

"It's three o'clock, and we are done. Do we want to see the rooms or wait until the girls get here and see them together?"

"Wait," everyone agreed at once.

Stella opened a bottle of wine and poured glasses then handed them around. She had just gotten to me when Ariel interrupted.

"Soph, do you have more flour? I was going to fry all this chicken"—she pointed to the several packs in the fridge—"as a homecoming meal for the girls."

"Crap, let me text Carter and have him pick up some."

"I need it before then. I just got this big ol' Fry Daddy going, I need it soon."

I looked to see if any of the girls were offering, but they all had their feet up and were already drinking their glasses of wine. "Okay, I'll just run up to the 7-11 real quick. Girls, keep drinking." I blew them kisses, grabbed my wallet out of my purse, and jumped into Carter's Jeep since he had the Land Rover with the girls' car seats. At 7-11, I grabbed five bags of flour since they only had the small one-pound bags. Then I added some salt and pepper, bottles of oil, and some M&M's for good measure.

On the way back, I was singing "Scars to Your Beautiful" at the top of my lungs, and I didn't notice the sheriff's car that pulled up behind me until his lights started flashing.

Shit.

I had probably been speeding. I flipped my turn signal and turned onto a side street that led back to my house before pulling over on the far shoulder of the road. I looked in my rearview mirror, but the officer didn't get out of the car right away. After another second, I reached for my wallet to grab my driver's license and then stopped.

"Please put your hands on the steering wheel so I can see them." The voice rang out from the PA.

I gripped the wheel and didn't move. Shit, this was Carter's Jeep. Since he was a deputy, didn't his license plate come back as a deputy? Wasn't there like a bro code or something about not pulling over other officers?

"Miss, please step out of the car and keep your hands where I can see them," the deputy ordered from his car's PA.

Okay, this was déjà vu, too similar to when I was eighteen

and Carter pulled me over. Only, it couldn't be him. He was driving my car and had the girls with him.

I got out and faced the sheriff's car as its door opened and a man got out, an older man, whom I didn't recognize.

"Ma'am, is this your vehicle?"

"No, sir, it's my boyfriend's."

"Well, I happen to know whose Jeep this is, and I know for a fact that he doesn't have a girlfriend."

"Sir, please just call Carter Lang. My name is Sophie—"

"Stop right there. Ma'am, you'll need to calm down."

"Sir . . ."

"Ma'am, I'm not going to ask you again. Now, turn around and put your hands behind your back."

"Sir, please," I pleaded but turned and put my hands behind my back as he had asked. "Sir, please, listen to me. This is Carter Lang's Jeep, I have permission to drive it; he has my car. You can call Deputy Piper Beaumont, she's at my house right now, or Sergeant Kayson Christakos, he's my cousin. But please just call Carter, he will tell you that I'm his girlfriend."

"That's the problem." I stilled as familiar callused fingers wrapped around my wrists and my lips turned into a smile. "He doesn't have a girlfriend, he has a fiancée, at least according to what she told the woman at the DMV." I spun around just as Carter reached into his pocket and pulled out a black velvet box before dropping to one knee. "Ten years ago, you sped into my life and, Sophie, you've never left. I know that we've only been back together a month, but it's been ten years to me. I'm never letting you go. Will you marry me?"

Throwing my hands over my face, I fought to find the words to express what I was feeling. I had everything and didn't have to sacrifice anything.

"Yes! Yes, I will marry you. Yes."

Carter cupped my face and pulled me in tight for a kiss.

Leaning me back against the Jeep, he swept his tongue inside my mouth. When he stepped back, he slid the ring, a beautiful solitaire surrounded by five colored stones, onto my finger.

"Why all the colors?"

"All of our birthstones—mine, yours, and the girls."

"It's perfect." I tilted my head back and gave Carter my lips again.

At the sound of a cough, I turned to see the older deputy still standing there.

"Thanks, Captain," Carter said before shaking the man's hand. After one last nod to me, the man was off.

"How'd you get here and where are the girls?"

"I was in the cruiser with him, and the girls were with your mom today. They are probably home by now."

Home. It was the world's greatest four-letter word. No, home was *almost* the best word. Love was definitely the greatest.

EPILOGUE

Carter

"Good grief, will you cool it, man?" Kayson said as he hiked his hip onto a table and sat. His brothers let out a laugh.

"Oh, just wait, Kayson. You are going to be just as crazy in a few months when you and Ariel get married," Damon, Kayson's oldest brother teased. "Welcome to the family, Carter."

Turning, I looked into the mirror and then paced the tiny vestibule room. "Why couldn't we just go to the Justice of the Peace? Or Vegas? Wait . . . never mind, I understand why no Vegas. But still—a Greek wedding. Do you know how many times I watched the movie *My Big Fat Greek Wedding* just so I'd know what to expect?"

They all let out a laugh.

"I swear that if anyone chases me around with a sheep's eyeball, I'm grabbing Sophie and the girls and we are going to Georgia. There isn't a waiting period there." I looked over to see Eli and Aiden, who were dressed in matching suits, just as their faces turned pale at the thought of eating eyeballs.

"No worries, the eyeballs are diced and sprinkled on the

food. You won't even know that you're eating them," Ian assured me. "Well, except for the fact that I just told you, so now you'll know."

I turned to give Kayson an is-he-shitting-me look, and he shook his head and then nodded. Fuck, what did that mean? A low rumble of laughter erupted, and I turned to see Tristan.

"Ian, you're an asshole." I punched his shoulder.

Everyone laughed, and in the small room, it sounded like a thunderclap.

"Seriously, though, do you have everything?" Tristan asked with all sincerity.

"Kayson has the rings. Harlow is carrying the book with the papers in it. God, I hope that Sophie is going to be okay with all this."

"Really, dude?" Kayson gave me a wry smile.

"Have any of you seen Sophie or the girls today?" I asked nervously. Just then, a knock sounded at the door, and my sister came in.

"You boys care if I have a few moments with my brother?"

They all cleared the room, Tristan being the last through the door. He thought he was sly as he reached for her hand, but he wasn't. "So, are Mom and Dad here?" I asked.

"Yep, they're already seated, and they both brought dates. So, all seems right in their worlds. How about you, how are you holding up?"

"I'm good. How's Sophie?"

"She's breathtaking." Stella leaned across the table she was sitting on and snagged a tissue from a box. "I love you so fucking much, but more than that, I'm proud of you. I can't believe that in just over six months, you've found the love of your life again, become a father three times over, and converted to Greek Orthodox."

"Hey, you converted with me. What's up with that anyway?"

"I figured that since my brother is Greek Orthodox, my best friend is Greek Orthodox, her soon-to-be husband and your soon-to-be wife are, then I might as well join in. But seriously, I love your life. I never thought I'd be at my brother's wedding or that I'd be an aunt, but I'm so happy and proud." She wiped away more tears and then waved her hands frantically in front of her eyes, trying to dry the wetness on her lashes.

I stepped toward her and pulled her in for a tight hug. "I love you, Stella. Now, go get my bride for me." When we broke away, I held my baby sister at arm's length and stared into her eyes, which were identical to mine. I wanted her to find love. Exactly like I had with Sophie.

She nodded and then left the room.

I took a few seconds to get myself and my thoughts together. This was all going to work out; I was doing the right thing. Not once had I wavered in my commitment to wanting to have Sophie for the rest of my life.

With one last look in the mirror, I straightened my navy-blue tie, then opened the door, and headed to the alter.

I stood in the front of the church, waiting, taking deep breaths, and listening to the piano. When Aiden and Piper began their walk down the aisle, followed by Everly and Eli, Vivian and Damon, Ian and Ariel, Tristan and Stella, and then finally, Kayson and Leo, my heart picked up speed with each pair.

Any moment, she was going to come down that aisle to be mine forever. The ladies were all in yellow dresses with the same dark blue accents as my tie. Well, everyone except Leo, who was in a yellow dress with more dark blue accents than the others. I liked how Sophie put both of our favorite colors together.

The music changed a bit, and Sophie's mom came out carrying Avril. Harlow, who was carrying a white book was next, and last was Gianna, who was carrying a basket full of white rose petals.

When Gianna saw me, she stopped tossing the petals into the air and ran toward me, shouting, "Daddy!" But Harlow stood in place, hollering for Gianna to come back and finish her job.

"Yep, she's just like Stella," Tristan whispered, and I laughed. Unfortunately, Stella heard that and stuck out her tongue.

When the music changed again, everything in me seemed to freeze, and even my heart ceased beating the moment I saw her.

She was stunning.

With her hand on her Uncle's, she glided down the aisle. Someone grabbed me, and I looked over my shoulder and saw Kayson's arm holding me back. I hadn't even realized that I had taken a few steps toward her. I was just so eager to get to her.

When they finally reached the front, I trembled as I held the woman of my dreams in my hands.

Father Alexios performed the service, and when he pronounced us husband and wife, I signaled for Dion to bring the girls up.

Taking the book from Harlow, I opened it and then turned the whole thing so Sophie could see the documents.

She slipped it from my grasp, and I picked up Gianna, who automatically reached for Sophie, but I held her back. Wrapping an arm around Harlow's shoulders and tugging her into me, I said, "We want you to sign those. Well, that's if you want to."

"If you sign them, then I can tell everybody that you're my mommy. I'll still have my mommy that I can't see, but I'll have you that I can see," Harlow explained.

Sophie had tears streaming down her face. "Is that what

you want, Harlow?" Harlow nodded. "How about you, *zoi mou?*" Sophie asked Gianna, calling her "my life."

"Mama."

That was it, that one word from Gianna had Sophie scribbling her autograph on three sets of legal documents. Today, we didn't become husband and wife, we became a family.

"This is almost perfect," Sophie said, pulling Harlow closer to her while I held on to Gianna.

"Almost?"

She turned and took Avril from her mother's arms and held her close so that all five of us were together. "Now it's perfect."

It's time to fall in love with the rest of the Christakos' brothers. Find Damon's story in ***Katy, My Impact***. Tap on the title to purchase or keep reading for a sneak peek.

Keep reading to find links to all of my books.

A WORD FROM DANIELLE

Thank you for picking up my book. It doesn't matter whether you have read one book of ten written by me, they all have some commonalities to them:

Strong women with attitude.

Alpha heroes who love them anyway.

And a strong bond of friendship that we all need in our lives.

The Iron Orchids, books 1 through 6, were my original series of romance novels. Each book can be read as a stand-alone. What connects the stories are the fact the same people appear and eventually each gets their own Happily Ever After.

So if you've read one then you are probably dying to read about the rest of the brothers and their missing cousin.

Read on to find sneak peeks from some of the books along with my suggested reading order.

Thank you again - Dani

Suggested Reading Order Including Excerpts

ORIGINAL IRON ORCHIDS, BOOKS 1 THROUGH 6
TAP THE LINKS TO FIND THE TITLE IN YOUR FAVORITE STORE

Ariel, Always Enough - Book 1
Sophie, Almost Mine - Book 2
Katy, My Impact - Book 3
Leo, Kiss Often - Book 4
Stella, Until You - Book 5
Christine, The Stars - Book 6

IRON ORCHIDS—BADGES SERIES, BOOKS 7 THROUGH 11

You met some of them in the Iron Orchids. Now these women motorcycle officers will ride into your heart.

Badges Prequel - Book 7
Sadie, Doctor Accident - Book 8
Bridget, Federal Protection - Book 9
Piper, Unlikely Outlaw - Book 10
Kat, Knight Watch - Book 11 (April 7, 2020)

IRON LADIES, BOOKS 1 AND 2

A whisper network of women. Women who help the wives of controlling men. You don't want to cross these ladies.

Adeline, Getting Even - Book 1
Sunday, Sweet Vengeance - Book 2

IRON HORSE, BOOKS 1 THROUGH 3

The love stories of three sisters who struggle to run a cattle ranch and to prove the strongest cowboys can be a girl.

London, Is Falling - Book 1
Paris, In Love - Book 2
Holland, At War - Book 3

SNEAK PEEK—KATY, MY IMPACT

Book 3, Original Iron Orchids

Chapter 1 - Katy

Just in case you were wondering, karma was pronounced as two blue lines meant you were pregnant. Oh, and its middle name was Ha-ha, Fuck You. But I wasn't bitter. No, I passed the blame to where it belonged . . . Disney, for my world of disillusions. Growing up, I never stopped to think about the *Little Mermaid* or why she had an entire song about her amazement at having legs. When in reality she should have been more shocked by the fact that she had a vagina.

But Cinderella truly boggled my mind. I was raised thinking she had it rough. In all actuality, the bitch had an entire movie, a prince, glass slippers, and for what? Being treated the way moms were treated every single fucking day of the year.

I should know, two weeks after I turned eighteen, I became a mom. Nothing made you grow up and face reality and all the lies you'd been fed in the fairy tales quite like telling your parents you were pregnant at the beginning of your senior year of high school.

"Mom. Mommmmm."

To me, she may as well have been screaming, "Cinderellaaa!"

I darted upstairs and into the master bedroom.

"What?"

"Mom. Look at the time." Bee pointed to her Kindle.

"Ah, crap. I'm sorry, I totally lost track of time. We gotta go. Hurry." Bee jumped out of bed and raced downstairs while I hurriedly rolled up the blankets, stacked our pillows on top of them, and tied a giant ribbon around the entire bundle for easy carrying. After taking one final glance around the room to make sure we left nothing behind, I turned and rushed back downstairs to join my daughter in our rehearsed morning routine. Reaching into my backpack, I pulled out Bee's toothbrush and toothpaste, and then handed them over before moving to our clothes duffle and pulling out an outfit for her.

"How about this?" I held up a pair of denim shorts and a University of Florida Gators shirt.

"Sure. Thanks, Mom." Bee took the clothes from me and closed the bathroom door. I rummaged through my bag, knowing full well she forgot the most important thing. "Mommy, can you bring me some toilet paper?" Tossing the roll in to her, I let out a laugh, the only time she called me Mommy anymore was when she needed something.

A few minutes later, we were ready. One more quick trek around to ensure the sink was spotless, the floor immaculate, and not a single blonde hair from either of us was left anywhere in the house, and we were ready.

"You've got your backpack with your homework?"

"Yes." She huffed, rolled her eyes, and pulled on her backpack as I grabbed our duffel, which was full of essentials like shampoo, conditioner, toothbrushes, toilet paper, and a change of clothing, and snagged the bundle of pillows and blankets.

Cracking open the back door, I stuck my head out and checked for anything out of the norm. Opening it wider, I gave Bee the go ahead. She dashed out, and I followed behind, making sure the door didn't completely catch as it closed. We headed straight into the woods where our car was safely parked and hidden.

I'd been putting off finding a new place, I hated change, but I hated the thought of getting caught even more. The property developers had changed the banners this week. The ones that once waved counting down the number of lots that had been available had been switched out for the red ones. Sold out. If that wasn't a sign that it was time to move on, then nothing was. All I could do was pray that the new subdivision would have a house for us to hide in.

We threw our duffels into the trunk, Bee holding her Kindle like the sacred item that it was to her as she headed to the front seat.

"Where do you want to go for breakfast? We're late, so it'll have to be drive-thru."

"Mickey D's is fine."

"Pancakes?" As if she'd want anything else.

"Duh."

"Duh." I shook my head at her and started the car.

Being a single parent without a college education and zero help in the world, money only went so far. I had to make some drastic decisions in life, some I was proud of, such as my beautiful girl sitting next to me, and some I was not so proud of . . .

But I had a bank account and was putting a small amount away to hopefully be able to afford the first, last, and security deposit somewhere. But the three thousand dollars I needed might as well have been three million dollars to me. With my car payment, phone bill, food, necessities, childcare for Bee when I was at work, plus a class at the community college so I could hopefully get a better-paying job someday didn't leave much in the bank.

I loved Orlando. Finding a job was super easy, but they were usually low-paying or had weird hours, which meant that childcare was outrageous.

I glanced in my rearview mirror to change lanes, and my stomach clenched. About three car lengths behind me was a black Charger. It wasn't the first time that I'd seen him, and I had a scary suspicion that I knew who it was. He was such a weasel but unfortunately I wasn't one-hundred percent positive that it was him, the windows were too dark. But the black Charger always seemed to appear out of thin air and had been doing so for just over a year. The first time I'd seen him began what I lovingly referred to now as, *musical houses*. That was the night Bee and I left the shelter and moved into the first house. I'd die before I'd allow him to get his hands on me or Bee.

"It's this weekend, right?" Bee asked, pulling me from my rising stress.

"This weekend for what?"

"Clothes shopping." Bee held out her hands as if the answer was obvious, and I nodded.

"Yep. Want to try Maitland or Winter Park this month?"

"Umm, Winter Park. Clothes there still have tags." Bee's eyes were wide as she told me this, reminding me new clothes were unheard of in our world.

God, I loved her so damn much, but seeing her face light up over having new clothes made me want to cry. I thought I'd made a game out of going to Goodwill. Every month, we'd take a few things to a consignment shop and sell them and then go to one of the Goodwill stores in the ritzy areas and dig for clothes that were practically new. Hell, I had even found a Burberry skirt there, and to think, I used to play outside in Burberry and didn't think twice about getting a stain.

Pulling into the turn lane with the rest of parents dropping their children off, I tried to think of what I could give up so Bee could have new clothes.

"Bye, Mom." Bee had her seatbelt unclasped.

"Give me a kiss," I said as I put my car in park in front of her school. "I have class today, so I'll pick you up late." I tapped her nose with my index finger when she leaned in to kiss my cheek. "Be a good bug." She slid out and slammed the door. That was when I noticed her Kindle in the door's side pocket. Rolling down the window, I hollered, "Hey, Bee bug, you forgot your Kindle." She raced back and grabbed it.

"Thanks, Mommy. Ms. Sophie is coming up to the community center today for book club."

"Okay, tuck it away. Love you." She turned and started to walk away. "Hey," I said, stopping her. She turned and gave me that smile that only Bee could give; it brightened the rainiest of days. It was us against the world. "You're the peanut to my butter." She blushed and headed to the school. A horn honked behind me aggressively and totally flipped my bitch switch. Glancing into the rearview mirror, soccer mom Suzy's smile reflected back. Of course, that wasn't really her name, but everyone knew this type of woman. They were always so fucking perfect, chaperoned all the school field trips, made homemade cupcakes for her kid's soccer team, and threw lavish birthday parties for her kid because she had a husband who worked and she stayed home. She was probably on some fucking tennis team as well.

"I'm going. I'm going. Hold your fucking horses. I was just saying goodbye to my kid." She honked again. "Okay, bitch. Do it again, and I'm getting out of my car." Not really, I wasn't ever brave enough. But I was tired, my kid had broken my heart over the thought of clothes with tags, and my patience was nonexistent. The woman laid on her horn and let it blare.

I put my car in gear and started rolling forward but had to stop when a little boy dashed in front of me. The bitch was still honking. Throwing my car into park, I grabbed my cup of coffee and got out.

"What's your problem, lady? Did you want me to run over the kid?"

"Well, we would have been passed him had you not dawdled for so long."

Dawdled? Who the fuck said dawdle? This crazy ass woman was probably late for a nail appointment. Or, I didn't know, maybe—colonics? She probably needed a massive cleaning because she was obviously full of shit.

"Whatever. Could you please move, I'm late for an appointment." Her voice was grating and nasally.

"I'm sorry. But please chill, there are kids."

"There is probably one less, looks like you may have eaten him." She waved her pointer finger at me before turning to the equally stuck up bitch sitting in the front seat next to her, who was wearing a tennis outfit. Yep, soccer mom Suzy and Tits Magee were late for the club.

Wanting nothing more than to chuck my coffee into their open car window and scream, I decided to be the adult, waved my fingers in the air, and walked back to my car. They might not know what waving the fingers meant, but I sure as hell did. My gesture was better than giving someone the bird; the bird was one finger. I was giving them the whole fucking flock.

I got to work, scanned my badge, and hauled ass down the hallway to my cubicle. I was in my seat and logging on with a minute to spare. I worked for Disney in the reservation center and helped people book their dream vacations, and I loved my job, the perks were even better. I couldn't give my daughter a lot, but my kid had known the ins and outs of every Disney park since we were able to go for free. The only drawback was the pay, which was why I was taking classes.

I smiled. After work today, I was headed to take the final exam in my accounting class, and that would put me one step closer to meeting my goals.

FIND ME

Website: www.daniellenorman.com

Official Iron Orchids Reading Group : www.daniellenorman.com/group

Sign up for Danielle's Newsletter and stay in the know
Newsletter: www.daniellenorman.com/news

Go to your App Store and download the app called Danielle Norman or visit
app.daniellenorman.com to download from the internet.

MEET DANIELLE

It is amazing what can happen over a glass of vodka. Danielle Norman knows all too well since that's how she was convinced to try writing a romance novel. A few more sips and seventy-thousand words later she was falling in love.

Her books have sold in more than two-hundred countries and her first book in the Iron Orchids series, *Ariel: Always Enough* has been downloaded more than two million times. It was a bestseller on Amazon and hit #1 on Apple Books and Barnes & Noble.

Danielle embraces her motto, *Romance with Attitude*.

ALSO BY DANIELLE

Books by Stella Lang

Stella Lang is the husband and wife writing duo of Rusty and Danielle Norman.

When reading books by Stella Lang you can always count on strong women, alpha men, hot sex (lots of hot sex), sarcasm, and a happily ever after that will curl your toes.

Stella Lang began as a sarcastic heroine in books by **Danielle Norman**.

Get your copy of ***Hard Blow***, Book 1 of the Orlando Suns series.

THANK YOU

- Editing by AW Editing
- Proofreading by Tandy Proofreads
- Proofreading Monique Tarver

💋 Oh, where do I start? Thank you, Ashley, for accepting a second manuscript from me. It's like playing lotto. I press send and wait to see if I get a reply that says, "Oh Fuck No, I'm not dealing with you again."

💋 Thank you, Sherry Howard, for being an awesome set of eyes. You catch all the tiny things that get missed.

💋 Thank you to Natasha, Kristen, Heather, Alexis, Jessica, Mandy, and Debbie for your willingness to do early reads, proofreads, and find your favorite quotes.

💋 Thank you to my awesome Stilettos, because you are fabulous, and stilettos make your ass look smaller.

💋 And to Effen Vodka- I hereby demand that you bring Salted Caramel Vodka back. I should not be expected to operate in my normal capacity sober. And if you name it Danielle's Salted Caramel Vodka, I won't object.

Printed in Great Britain
by Amazon